MW00978182

Tempting Secrets

A Tempting Nights Romance
Book One

MICHELLE WINDSOR

XO
Michelle Windsor

First published September 2018
Copyright © Michelle Windsor 2018
Published by
Windsor House Publishing
Cover design by Amanda Walker Design Services
Editing provided by Kendra's Editing and Book Services

This one is for my readers.
Thank you for all the love and support.

CHAPTER ONE

~Trey~

"Hey, man, you going to the gym with me or what?" I open one eye, snarling a warning to my roommate who's bouncing his sneakered foot on the end of my bed. "Cut the shit, asshole!" I sweep my bare leg across the mattress, knocking his foot off and causing him to lose his balance and almost fall. "I told you to give me ten minutes!"

"I've given you twenty, dude!" He walks out of my bedroom, slamming the door behind him, shouting, "I'm leaving in ten, with or without you, Trey!"

I drag myself into a sitting position, glance at the clock as I do, and groan when I see it's after nine. I have a ton of shit to get done today, and it looks like I've already wasted away a good chunk of my morning. I hate late night dates. Especially when they end with me pouring a drunk divorcee into bed, her begging me to join her because she's been so lonely since her husband left her for his secretary. Her words, not mine.

I run my hand down my face, trying to pull some of the sleep from my eyes, and get my ass in gear. Five minutes later, I'm standing in the living room, ready to head to the gym with my roommate Trick.

"It's about time, asshole," he grumbles, grabbing his gym bag off the table as he heads for the door.

"Sorry, man. Crap night." I shut the door after we both walk through, then we exit the building and head in the direction of the gym. It's New York City, so we pretty much walk or take the subway wherever we need to go.

"Who'd you have last night?" Trick asks as we walk.

"Lucy Greene," I state and roll my eyes.

"Try and sleep with you again?"

"Yep, but not until she had three martinis in her, and then you know you can't tell her a damn thing. Literally had to peel her off me in order to try to get out of her apartment." I shake my head at the memory.

"You need to tell Cory to take her off your rotation. You don't need to deal with that shit."

I nod my head and frown. "She pays so damn well that it's hard to red light. Ya know what I mean, man?"

He just nods his head. Trick knows better than anyone what I'm talking about because we both work at the same place: Temptations Escort Agency. And, yeah, it's exactly what it sounds like. We're paid escorts. Dates for hire. We are arm candy, paid to satisfy the whims of our client. And, no, we aren't prostitutes. Money will get you a lot but some of us have our limits. We're officially hired to escort a woman, or a man in some cases, to whatever event she or he requests. It could be a wedding, a simple dinner date for company, a not so simple dinner date where she's trying to make an ex jealous, charity balls, funerals, or pretty much anything you can think of.

Cory manages Trick and I and sets up all our encounters. She knows what our limits are, and if there's any question, she forwards the request to us for approval. *Officially*, we're only paid for our escort services. There's no money exchanged with Temptations for sex. That would be illegal, after all. But it happens. All the time. Because sometimes the money is too good to turn down, and let's face it, we're not doing this because we need a date. And in my case, some of us *need* the money.

I still owe thirty grand on my tuition for the physician's assistant program I'm enrolled in, and the sooner I get it paid off, the less I have hanging over my head. I start my clinical practicum in three weeks, and even though I'll be getting paid, it's not going to be anywhere near enough to pay my rent in the city, my tuition bill, and my living expenses.

But, even I have my limits; Mrs. Greene is case-in-point. She's a beautiful, rich divorcee who likes nothing more than to throw her money at me, but she's still in love with her soon-to-be ex-husband. Adding me into the mix will just make things harder for her. Even if she's not able to see that yet, I am.

We reach the gym and enter to the sound of metal clanking and the smell of testosterone thick in the air. Trick and I don't say much during our workout. These are a matter of necessity, not enjoyment, and some days we just want to get through it and move on to the next thing. We've known each other since we served in the army together; me as a medic and him as a medivac chopper pilot.

He could probably make bank doing private helicopter tours or as a medivac pilot here, but he was gutted when his chopper was shot down and everyone but him died in the crash. Hasn't been able to fly since. Unlike me, Trick doesn't have many limits. Working at the service allows him to be anyone but himself and get paid for it, making it easier for him to try to forget what happened overseas.

Trick and I push through a standard workout and then take a quick shower. We meet back in the lobby after we're dressed to figure out the rest of our day.

"You have a job tonight?" I ask as I approach him sitting at the juice bar drinking a protein shake.

He gives me a wicked grin. "I've got Grace Mathers tonight."

I roll my eyes as I sit beside him. "Better you than me. She's a friggin wildcat."

"That's what I like about her. I never know what she's gonna surprise me with next, but it's never dull." He gulps down the rest of his drink. "What do you have going on?"

"Someone new. Single woman wants a date for a charity event. Seems like an easy night." I turn my attention to the staff behind the counter and order myself a shake. "I have to go pick my tux up from the cleaners. Haven't needed it in a couple weeks."

"Okay, I'm going to take off then. Maybe hit Dark Pleasures on my way home and see if I can't find something special for Ms. Mathers." His eyebrow raises as one side of his mouth cocks up in a salacious grin.

"Yeah, have fun with that. I'll catch you back at our place later."

He stands, slaps a hand on my shoulder in goodbye, and walks off just as my shake is placed in front of me. I nod in thanks, grab my phone out of my duffel, and go through my messages as I drink my breakfast. Nothing too exciting, except for an email from Mrs. Greene, forwarded by Cory, expressing embarrassment and apologies for her behavior the evening before. I cringe a little reading the desperation in her email but can't help but feel sad for this woman who is clearly feeling so insecure over her husband's infidelities.

I finish up my shake, leave a five on the counter and head to the cleaners to grab my tux for this evening.

Seven hours later, my town car pulls up beside an address in the *very* good part of town. I step out of the car, make my way into the building and stop at the concierge desk, where I'm greeted by a middle-aged man in a sharp uniform.

"Good evening, sir. Can I help you this evening?"

"Maddox Stone, here for Karen Perry. She's expecting me."

"Of course, one moment, sir, while I ring her."

I take a few steps around the grand marble foyer and admire the paintings hanging on the wall as he announces my arrival to my date. I'm not familiar with the artist, but it's definitely from the impressionist era and simply stunning.

"She'll be down in just a moment, Mr. Stone," the concierge calls from his desk.

I wave my hand in acknowledgement as I stop to absorb the beauty in one particular painting. It's a simple image actually; a single boat in a pond, with a single occupant. A woman. But on shore are three smaller images. Her children? I'm not sure and the mystery of it has me investigating every speck of paint on the canvas for some kind of clue to the answer.

I'm not sure how long I've been staring at the painting, but it must have been for several minutes because I'm startled when a hand touches me on the elbow. "Excuse me, Mr. Stone?"

I turn and come face to face with a much older woman. My brows raise slightly in surprise as my gaze sweeps from her face and down her body, which is sheathed smartly in a navy-blue satin gown. "Yes?"

She laughs lightly, her eyes twinkling in delight as she replies, "Karen Perry."

My brows arch higher, and I fight to keep my mouth closed as surprise catches me off guard for just a moment. She must be at least eighty years old. *This is my date?* I recover quickly and plant a smile on my face and nod. "I'm so sorry. Nice to meet you."

"Not exactly what you were expecting?" Eyes that mirror the color of her dress light up in mischief as one side of her mouth crooks up in a slight smirk.

Again, completely caught off guard. "Er, well, I—"

Her hand comes up and rests gently on my forearm. "Blame it on that damn Caroline Beaumont!" She pulls at my arm gently and starts walking in the direction of the lobby exit. "Every event

I go to, she is rubbing her son's accomplishments in my nose, knowing full well I never had any children with Astor." She pauses mid-step and looks in my direction. "Astor is, well, was my husband. He passed a year ago."

"Oh, I'm very sorry." I'm sincere in my condolences, seeing the sadness that washes across her features upon saying his name.

She pats my arm, her lips pursing downward for just a moment. "Thank you, dear. He's missed." She starts walking again, switching topics as quickly as one flips a pancake. "Anyway, Astor and I met quite late in life, and as such never had children of our own. And Caroline just loves to remind me of that. I've had enough!"

We've reached the town car, and after a nod in the driver's direction, the rear door is opened and I assist Mrs. Perry into the back seat. I move to the opposite side and settle myself in beside her. "I'm sorry, please continue."

She holds her finger up to me and then addresses my driver. "Dear, we're going to Gotham Hall on Broadway. Do you know it?"

"Yes, ma'am." Gene looks at me in the rearview and I nod in approval, his indication to begin our journey.

I shift my gaze back to my *date* who has lowered her finger and has both hands clasped demurely in her lap, a look of curiosity on her face.

"What is it?"

"Are you always the boss?" Again, the look of mischief plays in her eyes.

I chuckle and run a hand over my chin at her observation. "Technically, you're the boss, but Gene does like to make sure I'm on board with all decisions."

A smile pulls at the wrinkles around her mouth, making them smoother. "I think you're going to do quite nicely as my nephew."

"Nephew?" My head cocks. *This is a new one.*

"Yes, nephew. Tonight, you're my sister's son, here in town for a visit." She nods her head matter-of-factly like I should already be aware of this fact. "You didn't think I wanted to have sex with you, did you?"

I can't contain the laughter that erupts straight from my belly at her brazen question. She has no filter and I love it. "Mrs. Perry, I've learned to always expect the unexpected."

She chuckles back. "Well, I'm certainly not expecting that. And if we're going to pull this off, you're going to have to call me Aunt Karen."

"Got it." I wipe the smile off my face and get down to business. "What else do I need to know?"

"Well, let's see. I need you to be successful, of course." Her eyes travel over my face, studying it for a moment. "Exactly how old are you? I asked the agency for someone in their twenties, intelligent and good looking. They got the good-looking part down."

"I'm twenty-eight. Will that do?" I'd have to thank Cory for putting me in the intelligent, good-looking bucket.

"That will do." She nods and then waves a hand around the car. "Now, is this all you do?"

I raise my brows in question. "This?"

"You know, date the ladies?" She states it like it should be so obvious to me.

I chuckle and then answer the question. "I was in the Army as a medic for six years and have been in PA school for the last year. I start my clinical rounds in a couple weeks."

"PA school?"

"Physician's Assistant. It's sort of like a step down from an M.D. I can see patients, write scripts, work in a hospital or a doctor's office ." I watch as she absorbs this information, her head bobbing up and down in understanding as I speak. "This is what I do to help pay for that."

"The Army didn't pay for your schooling?"

"A good part of it but not all of it. There's still living expenses, books, clothing."

"Why not just go to medical school?"

It's a question I get a lot. Why a Physician's Assistant degree? Why not medical school? It's an easy answer for me. "Money. And time. Getting your M.D. is six more years of school and training. It's an expense I don't have the luxury to afford, and honestly, becoming a PA satisfies my need to be able to take care of people."

She places her fingers over mine and gives me a warm smile. "I wasn't judging, dear. I was just curious." She gives my hand a squeeze then. "So, PA it is then. It won't be too hard at all for me to brag about you!"

I return her smile. "Okay, let's get some of the facts down then. My mother's name? Where do I live? My name? How do you want to play this?"

"Oh, you're so good at this!" Her mouth pulls into a wide smile. "My sister's name is Kathy, and is your mother. She's real, and is retired and living in Palm Springs with her husband, your father, Thomas. You grew up in Los Angeles where, by the way, your father worked as a trauma surgeon at UCLA Medical Center." She looks at me and pauses. "So far, so good?"

"Yep. Kathy and Tom, Palm Springs, LA, UCLA. What about me? Am I Maddox? Do they really have a son?"

She frowns. "Unfortunately, no. They have two daughters. But it doesn't matter. Is Maddox Stone your real name?"

"What do you think, Mrs. Perry?" I give her a sardonic rise of my eyebrow.

"Aunt Karen," she corrects. "Yes, well, Maddox Stone does sound like something a news reporter or an escort would use." She chuckles at her own joke, looking at me as she does. "Can you tell me your real name?"

"I'm not supposed to." I purse my lips in thought and then nod my head. "But I don't anticipate you trying to stalk me or cause me any harm."

"Oh, dear, I would never!" she exclaims.

I smile warmly at her and nod, because I know she wouldn't.

"It's Trey. Trey Riley." It feels strange telling a client my real name. It's a first for me. Something I've never done and, quite frankly, am not supposed to do. But Karen Perry feels the furthest from a client than anyone I've ever been assigned to.

"You're kidding me!" Her eyes are wide and her mouth falls open.

"No..."

"This must be fate or kismet or something like that." She places her hand back over mine and leans forward like she's about to tell me the secret of the century. "Tom and Kathy's last name is Riley."

CHAPTER TWO

~Charlotte~

"Thank God this day is over!" Raising my hand over my head, I clench it in a fist and pump it in the air in triumph. "Longest damn shift ever! But we made it, girls!" I turn, smiling broadly at my two closest friends, Kinsley and Gabby. "Cocktails?"

"Yes!" they both reply in unison.

"O'Malley's?" Gabby suggests. It's one of the local watering holes close to the hospital that many of us frequent after our shifts. We just finished a grueling twelve hours and have the next three days off, so we are more than ready for a little unwinding.

"Yes!" Kinsley and I reply together this time, all of us breaking into giggles. We cross the street and stroll arm in arm down the sidewalk, recounting our day of hell.

"Did you see the man that came in with the knife stuck in the back of his head?" Kinsley exclaims. "I mean, the dude walked in! How is it even possible he was still alive, let alone walking and talking?"

"Yes! I saw him! Just crazy!" We continue gossiping about the many patients that invaded the emergency room that day as we continue the short walk to the bar, laughing as we pass through the entrance into the crowded space. It's almost eight pm and, therefore, prime drinking time for many.

Gabby, who stands just a few inches shy of six feet, has no problem parting the crowd as she moves forward. Kinsley and I stay close behind and almost squeal in delight when we see her snag a booth that a couple is leaving, each of us sliding in after her to sit.

"Well done, Gabs!" My face lights up with a smile. I see the waitress walk by, so I raise my hand to flag her down. She nods her head, lifting her finger to indicate that she'll be with us in a minute. Sure enough, a moment later, she's at the booth and takes our order of three well-needed cocktails and a basket of fries.

"What are your plans for the next three days, Miss Charlotte?"

"Ugh! Don't call me that. It's so southern belle. You know I prefer Charlie," I huff out at her. "And, sleep! At least for the first day!" I groan out to Kinsley. "Six days on has nearly killed me." These are twelve-hour shifts, many of them running over by an hour or two by the time shift changes and patient transfers occur. When I finally get home and unwind, there aren't many hours left for actual sleeping. Both friends nod in complete understanding. "What about you girls?"

Gabby scans the room before returning her gaze to us, her brows raising suggestively. "If I can find a willing candidate, I'd be more than happy to spend the next twelve hours with a man between my legs."

Kinsley slaps a hand against Gabby's shoulder and shoves her playfully. "You are such a little slut, Gabs!"

"Enjoying sex does not make me a slut, Kinsley. It just means I know what I like. Plus, we're only in our twenties once, my friends." She lets out a naughty giggle and continues. "Perhaps if you didn't marry the first guy you fell in love with, you'd under-stand how a little variety only makes the menu so much more appealing."

Kinsley's cheeks turn a light pink as she bites her lip, her eyes casting downward. "Oh, don't worry, Gabs, Tristan is the master of variety." Kinsley is the only one of us who is married. She met her husband, Tristan, when she was in nursing school, and it was love at first sight. Of course, he was one of her instructors, which made things slightly difficult for a semester, but that's a story for another time.

"Now who's the slut?" Gabby replies playfully, all three of us breaking into laughter. "Speaking of variety," Gabby's gaze zeros in on me, "when's the last time you got laid, Charlie?"

"Oh, no!" I wave my hand in dismissal. "We are so not going there! I'm so done with men. Done! Done! Done!" I slap my hand on the table to make my point final.

"Oh, come on, Charlie! You can't let a couple bad eggs ruin the rest of the basket for you," Kinsley, ever the romantic, replies.

"A couple?" I snort. "It's been more than a couple, and you both know it." I glare at them both as I recount the last few disasters I'd been involved in. "The doctor who apparently liked to provide regular *exams* to half the surgical nursing staff, the bartender who ended up being married, and how about the vet? He was the worst of the bunch!" I shake my head roughly. "N-O! I am staying clear of men."

"But don't you get," Kinsley lowers her voice to a whisper, "horny?"

"That's what vibrators are for, my friend. And B.O.B. is always there when I need him. He never cheats, isn't married, and most certainly doesn't like animals!"

Another round of giggles ensues before Kinsley continues. "But the human factor, the touching and the hugging and the kissing? I would miss that."

I sigh, my shoulders rising and falling in a shrug. "I do miss that. But when I weigh the pros with the cons, B.O.B. wins right now." I take a long sip of my drink before I continue. "I mean, don't get me wrong. There's nothing I'd like more than to find a good, decent guy, but it just doesn't seem to be in the cards right now."

Gabby pats me on the arm, a sympathetic smile tugging the corners of her mouth up slightly. "So, just love 'em and leave like I do, kiddo. The catch and release program is working just fine for me."

We break out into another round of giggles before I respond. "Oh, you know me, I'm just not that kind of girl!"

"Well, the kind of girl you are now ain't working out so well for you either, is it?" she responds tartly but not unkindly.

I laugh and nod my head in resignation. "Ain't that the truth."

The waitress wanders by and we ask for another round, the first one already making me feel a little buzzed, but I'm enjoying the warm fuzzy feeling after the last few days of hard work. Gabby lifts her chin in the direction of the bar. "Look at that hottie, Charlie. Doesn't just looking at him get you all warm and tingly? I mean, can you imagine what a few hours with him would do for your soul?" She raises her eyebrows suggestively, one side of her mouth quirking up, before taking a long sip of her drink, eyes glued in the direction of the bar.

Of course, I have to turn and look. Yep. He's definitely hot, and his friend isn't so bad either. I watch as he turns, leans his elbows back on the bar, and then sweeps his gaze over the patrons in the bar, his long, lean body relaxed as he does. I flinch, actually feel my muscles tighten when his eyes latch onto mine, and a slow, sexy smile spreads across his face. My skin instantly heats from the intensity of his stare, which to me is a red flag, so I turn my attention quickly back to my friends.

"Oh my God. Did you see him look at me?" I shake my head in disbelief, my hair swishing around my face as I do. "That's what I'm talking about. That is just dangerous. I don't need any of that!"

"Ha!" Gabby huffs. "You may think you don't need any of that, but I saw how you just reacted. You *want* some of that!"

"Nope. Not happening," I spit out. "Been there, done that. Not

13

going there again." I lift my head ever so slightly and take the quickest peek through my lashes at him, just to confirm that he's nothing but trouble. "He's just another mistake waiting to happen."

"Well, if you aren't going to make that mistake, I think I might." Gabby stands to her full height, shakes her long, black hair around her shoulders, and saunters toward the bar. I don't know how she does it. I watch in awe as, in less time than it takes for her to lean against the mahogany, the friend of sexy guy is moving to stand next to her and offers to buy her a drink. I snort and am about to look away but stop as I feel eyes on me.

I shift my gaze to the left and freeze when they lock onto sexy guy still staring at me. His brow raises the slightest bit as he cocks his head to me in invitation. Oh, how I'd like to stand and deliver right now, but nope, not doing it. I know exactly how this will end, and I'm not going there again. I shake my head at his request and break his piercing hold by turning back to Kinsley. "So, what do you and Josh have planned on your days off?"

"Shut the hell up!" My mouth hangs open as I listen to Gabby describe in detail the night she spent with sexy guy's friend. I know now that his name is Trick, and it sounds like he's got a bag full of them based on what she's telling me.

"You shut the hell up! It was some of the best sex I've ever had!" She doesn't even have the decency to blush as she continues telling me about how turned on she got when he asked her to spank him. With a leather belt. A little more information than I need to know about my friend, so I raise my hand.

"Okay, I've heard enough." Apparently, so has our waitress, whose cheeks are a bright red as she sets my breakfast plate in front of me. I offer a small smile in apology as she scurries away.

It's Tuesday, two days into our three days off, and Gabby, Kinsley, and I have met for breakfast and some shopping.

"I'm just saying, don't knock it 'til you try it." She picks up her fork and stabs some fried potatoes onto it before shoving them into her mouth, which of course is turned up in a naughty smirk.

"Ugh," I moan out. "You are too much, Gabrielle." I stand up and push my chair back. "I've got to use the ladies. I'll be back."

"So, guess what?" Gabby gleams wickedly at Kinsley.

"I'm afraid to even ask, but what?"

Gabby leans in closer to Kinsley and, in a hushed voice, starts talking quickly. "Okay, so I have to say this really fast before Charlie comes back, but I have an idea!"

Kinsley's eyes roll up as she shakes her head. "No. Whatever it is, if you're whispering, I know it can't be good!"

"Hush!" Gabby's hand reaches out and latches onto one of Kinsley's arms. "Trick is an escort! And he has a friend that I think we should set Charlie up with. You remember Mr. Sexy from the bar the other night? How hot she thought he was?"

"Wait! What?" Kinsley sits up straight, her mouth open in a small 'O' before it closes and she continues. "Did you hire Trick to sleep with you? I'm so confused!"

"Keep up, Kins!" She waves her hand to indicate Kinsley should move closer again. "I picked him up that night. He wasn't working. But he *and* his friend are both escorts for some placed called Temptations. Of course, his friend asked about Charlie, because, duh, she's gorgeous."

"Okay, so he wants to see her?" Kinsley is whispering now as well.

"I don't know. I mean, probably. Who wouldn't want to see her." Gabby rolls her eyes dramatically as she waves a hand in the air dismissively. "But you know Charlie will never agree to a date. She's anti-men right now. Especially dating. And especially if she finds out what he does for a living."

"Yep, that's for sure." Kinsley nods. "So, I don't understand. What do you want to do?"

"I think we should hire him to seduce her! One night of bliss to make her forget about all the other losers taking up space in her head." Gabby is grinning widely, nodding her head in excitement at her own idea. "Trick said he'd set it up so we could pay a minimum fee. I mean, he was clearly into her anyway."

"Oh, Gabby, I don't know if this is such a good idea. I mean, do we really want to trick her like that?"

"Well, we need to do something, Kins, or she's going to turn into a nun. Besides, it would just be for one night. A little fun to break the bad guy spell. We don't want her marrying a damn escort, for Christ's sake!" Gabby looks up, eyes growing momentarily wide, and then shifts so she's sitting up straight again.

"What are you two whispering about?" Charlie pulls her chair back out and sits across from them, a curious look in her eyes.

"Oh, nothing, just sharing a little more about Trick and his talents," Gabby replies without hesitation.

"You're still on that subject?" Charlie groans and shakes her head. "You have a one-track mind!"

"But it's such a fun track to be on!" Gabby retorts, all three girls breaking into a chorus of laughter as they finish their brunch and head off to do some shopping.

CHAPTER THREE

~Trey~

"You're kidding me, right?" I run a hand through my wet hair and then wipe it on the towel that's wrapped around my waist. I've just finished showering in preparation for a client I have in an hour.

"What's the big deal? You saw her at the bar and thought she was hot." Trick's sitting on the sofa in our living room, clad in just a pair of boxers, his fingers flicking continuously on the game controller he has in his hands. "We can set it up for one of your off nights and it will be all cash under the table."

"I see tons of girls in bars that I think are hot. That doesn't mean I want them as clients. And because it feels wrong. This shit should go through Cory." I walk through the living room and into my bedroom, speaking louder as I go, making sure shit-for-brains can still hear me. "Why the hell does she need her friends to buy her a date anyway? She was gorgeous." I close my eyes and recall the way her brown shaggy locks framed her delicate face. Eyes were wide as a doe's, the color of them appearing just as soft.

"Gabby said something about a basket of bad eggs or some shit like that." His voice trails from the other room as he yells a few profanities at the television.

"Who the fuck is Gabby?" I pull on a pair of fitted boxer briefs and then move to stand in my doorway so I can hear him better.

"Her friend. The one I went home with the other night." He lets out a long sigh, tosses the controller on the table, and rises, turning in my direction as he does. "Keep up, will ya? And, seriously, what the fuck difference does it make to you anyway? It's just another date. Can you just do this one solid for me? I told her I'd help her out."

"When did you start giving a shit about what anyone else needs?" I blow back at him. I can't remember the last time Trick did anything for anyone other than himself.

"Because she's fucking incredible in bed and I'd like to get myself another piece of that shit if I can." He tilts his head, a devilish grin splitting his lips in two as if this should be so obvious to me.

"Do you ever think with anything besides your goddamn dick?" Wet drops sprinkle down around my shoulders as I shake my head laughing. "Fine. What do you need me to do?"

"Shit! You'll do it? Really?" Trick's grin grows wider as I nod my head.

I shrug. "Like you said, it's just another date. And another few hundred bucks is always welcome." *Plus, I wouldn't mind getting a closer look at those sweet, brown eyes.* "Just let me know where and when."

"Roger that." He walks by me, slapping me on the shoulder as he passes. "I'll talk to Gabby and find out when her next day off is and we'll set something up."

"And she doesn't know about it?" I turn and follow him into the kitchen.

"Nope. They just want you to show her a good time and remind her that all men aren't complete assholes." I watch as he reaches into the fridge and pulls out a beer. "You want one?"

I shake my head. "Can't. Date in an hour." I draw in a breath and exhale slowly. "I hate the secretive shit. It always comes back and bites you in the ass."

"I think it just adds to the fucking fun of it all." He raises the bottle and then takes a long sip.

"So, am I Maddox or am I Trey?"

He smiles wickedly. "You're Maddox, man. On duty. This is a one-time thing. Just remind her how fucking awesome a good man can be."

"I can do that." I grin, one brow raising suggestively. "What's her name again?"

"Jesus Christ, man. I've told you three times. Gabby."

"Not her, asshole. The girl you want me to *remind*."

"Charlene? Cheryl?" He walks past me and heads back toward the living room. "Something like that. I'll find everything out and let you know."

"Okay." I walk behind him and then detour to my bedroom to finish getting ready for my client. She's a regular, who just likes someone pretty on her arm for dinner now and then. It's nice knowing what to expect of the evening and of my client, unlike nights with Mrs. Greene.

~Charlotte~

"So, what if I don't want to go?" I toss back over my shoulder at Gabby as I wheel a patient down the hall for an x-ray. She's tight on my heels, trying to convince me to go to an event she's required to be at.

"Of course, you want to go!" she huffs out. "What else do you have to do this weekend? And, besides, I really don't want to go alone. You know how I feel about Mother's parties."

Gabby's parents are rich. And I don't mean, 'a house in the Hamptons and keep a driver' rich. They are, 'houses in Europe,

Aspen, on both coasts, New York City, *and* the Hamptons, with cars and drivers in each location' rich. And, lucky her, she's their only child. You can imagine how thrilled her parents were when she announced she was opting out of the family business to go to nursing school instead. She does appease them from time to time by visiting regularly *and* by attending functions when requested. This is where I come in because she detests going to any family gathering by herself and always wants to drag me along.

"Please. With a cherry on top?" she pleads and then sweetens the pot. "I'll take you out and buy you a brand-new dress and shoes!"

"Honey, if you don't want to go, I will," the elderly woman in the wheelchair states. "I haven't gotten a new dress in ages."

Gabby and I both laugh out loud. I pat my patient gently on the shoulder. "Unfortunately, I do think that ankle might be broken, Mrs. Hughes, so dancing may be off your list of activities for a few weeks."

"Is that a yes then?" Gabby asks, hands clenched expectantly in front of her.

"Fine." I stick my tongue out at her. "You win. But I'm buying the most expensive outfit I can find!"

"Whatever. I'm charging it to Daddy's card anyway." She sticks her tongue right back out at me, grins, and then places a quick kiss on my cheek before turning back in the direction we came. "Thank you!" She glances over her shoulder and calls out, "We're gonna find you something sexy!"

An hour later, I'm sitting at the nurses' station updating charts when Gabby plops down in the seat next to me. She pulls out her phone, swipes the screen a few times, and then shoves it in front of my face. "I see you in this."

When my eyes finally focus, it's on a barely-there red dress with a price tag of thirty-four hundred dollars. I sputter and then push the phone away in disbelief. "Are you crazy? That dress is ridiculously expensive! And there's hardly anything to it!"

She turns the phone, looks at the picture of the dress again like it's the first time she's seen it, and then looks back at me. "It would look fabulous on you. I mean, you're so petite, and with your barely-there boobs, it's perfect. You wouldn't need a bra at all, which is, again, perfect with the back of this dress."

I roll my eyes. Hard. "No."

"Well, we are finding you something spectacular. That's all there is to it." She shrugs and begins scrolling through more pictures on her phone.

"What's your obsession with finding me a dress?" I scoff at her.

"Because I have hundreds in my closet. It's fun to shop for someone else." She looks over at me and pushes her bottom lip out in a fake pout. "Can't you just let a girl have a little fun?"

I chuckle and then reach out to squeeze her cheeks in my hands. "Fine. Have it your way. But not red. And not blue! We live in these blue scrubs!"

"Okay, okay. But, I'm just saying, you look fabulous in red." Gabby shrugs her shoulders and continues musing. "I mean, with your coloring and your tan."

"But it's summer now and I want something light and pretty."

"Oh, I actually have something I think will work perfect for you then!" She sits up straighter and giggles in delight. "I saw it last week when I was in Chanel."

"Chanel?" My mouth falls open before quickly forming a smile. "Well, I mean, if Daddy's buying." We both break into a little fit of giggles. "Where's the event and what's it for this time?"

"Oh, I don't know, some children's charity, and it's at the Connecticut house." She sets her phone down as she spits out her next words quickly. "I know we can take the train, but Daddy's sending a car for us at noon, and we can spend the night there." I go to speak, but she raises her hand to stop me. "And, before you even protest, just don't. I am not sitting in a stuffy train car for forty-five minutes because it makes you feel better about not spending my father's money."

"Fine," I respond.

"Fine?" Gabby's voice is full of disbelief. "Just like that?"

"Yep." I nod. "I am not lugging Chanel on the train. And, seriously, what else do I have to do this weekend?"

"Wow. That was easy," she says, slightly dazed.

"I'm picking my battles, Gabs." I nod my head in defeat and give her a small but genuine smile. "You win this one."

She smiles back at me. "It should be a really great time actually. It's outside on the back lawn, and with the water and the weather, it should be beautiful."

"Sounds perfect," I say, honestly looking forward to the night now.

"And, who knows, Charlie, maybe you'll even find yourself a man!"

"Yeah, we both know that's the last thing I want."

"Isn't that when it happens, when you expect it the least?" She giggles and then her face grows serious as she continues to look at me. The corners of her mouth pull up just a little and then she winks at me, a look of confidence twinkling in her eyes, just like she looks when she has a secret.

CHAPTER FOUR

~Trey~

"You're sure there's no other day we can do this?" I let out a frustrated huff of air as I continue pumping the barbell of weights over my chest. Trick's standing over me, spotting the bar in case I get tired. "I mean, for me to even have a Saturday off is rare. I was kind of looking forward to a relaxing weekend before I start my clinicals."

I finish the set, and after settling the bar back in its hooks, I swivel to sit up on the bench. I look up at Trick and pause when I see a strange look on his face. "What?"

He shuffles his sneakered feet back and forth before looking me in the eye, a cautious expression on his face. "I may have asked Cory to make sure she kept this weekend clear for you."

Realization about why I actually have a free weekend dawns, and I stand in anger. "What the fuck, man! On a weekend I could have actually been making some real money, you arranged it so I have to schlep out to goddamn Connecticut to try and woo some charity case, just so you can get laid again by some chick who rocked your socks off!"

Trick throws his hands up in defense and takes a step back. "Whoa! Chill out, man. You just said it was nice to have a weekend off. And what's more relaxing than the Connecticut seaside, especially with a hot girl?"

"Yeah, a hot girl some other girl is paying me to seduce for a night. It's not relaxing if I'm on the job, asshole." I step forward and punch him hard in the arm. "And I don't appreciate you screwing with my schedule. Cory's going to hear about this."

"Ow!" Trick rubs his arm, sits on the bench I abandoned, and begins a set of chest presses. "Don't blame Cory. I told her you wanted a weekend off. She has no idea about any of the other stuff."

"You really are an asshole." I push down on the bar so he can't lift it off his chest and smirk down at him, liking the position I have him in. "You know that, right?"

"Yeah, yeah!" He grunts and pushes back against my hold on the weights. "Now, get this the hell off me!"

I help him pull the weights up and back onto the holding ledge, glaring at him the entire time. He ignores my blatant attempt to intimidate him and instead sports a cocky grin that lifts his eyebrows. "And, for the record, that girl didn't just rock my socks off; she rocked my whole fucking world. I need a little more of that."

I roll my eyes as I sit back down on the bench to do another set. "I don't even want to know how, you sick mother fucker."

Trick rolls his shoulders and scoffs. "Takes one to know one."

I shake my head as I lift the bar and begin my set. "So, what's the plan with the girl? Tell me again."

"Yeah, so Gabby and her friend will be at this charity function her parents are having in Connecticut. There'll be lots of people at the event, so throwing you into the mix is easy. I guess the girls are spending the night there, so you should have plenty of opportunity to get yourself known and do your thing."

"And tell me again why you can't come with me? It would sure make things a lot easier." Trick finishes his set, clanging the bar back in place, and then sits up, sweat running down his temples. He reaches for his towel sitting on the floor next to us and uses it to wipe his face. "Because, unfortunately, I do have to work this weekend. And, besides, it would look like a complete set-up if I showed up with you. Too match-makery, and Gabby said that the last thing this chick wants is another set-up."

"Oh, but this kind of arrangement is okay?" I grunt out in response.

"You and your amazing charm will have her thinking it's completely organic. Gabby just wants her to have a little fun with a guy and not have him fuck her over afterwards."

I look at him, my lips pulling down into a frown. "And what if you want to keep seeing this Gabby? You don't think our paths are going to cross?" I pace back and forth in front of him. "It just seems wrong to screw with this girl's emotions like this."

"First of all, when have you known me to see a girl more than three times? Ever." He rises and throws the towel back on the floor as he walks over to grab a twenty-five-pound dumbbell off the rack. "And, second of all, the idea is to make the girl feel special for a night. That's it. Nothing more. You're not going to make her breakfast in the morning or share your fucking number with her after. Just show her a good time for the night. Get her to realize there are some nice guys still left in the world. Keep it what it's supposed to be, and things will be fine."

"You better be right about this." I walk over beside him, grab a dumbbell of the rack, and mimic his movements. "The date usually hires me. Expects me to be there. Tells me what they want and need. No secrets. I'm not used to doing things this way. And you know I hate the unexpected. I don't want to trick this girl into something. Feels shitty. Like I'm using her."

"Hopefully, she'll be using you," he replies sarcastically and then lets out a long breath and turns to me. "Look, if you're that uncomfortable about it, I can tell Gabby to forget it. I don't want to make you do something you don't want to do." I watch as he shrugs his shoulders before he continues. "I saw you checking her out at the bar and thought you were into her so assumed it was a no-brainer."

I look at him for a second, his little speech reminding me why he's been my friend for so long, and then give him a small grin. "I said I'd do it. Relax."

"Now who's the asshole?" He laughs and shoves me back playfully. "You sure, man?"

"Yep. I'm good." I sigh under my breath in resignation. "What's her name again?"

~Charlotte~

"Charlie!" Gabby gasps as I walk out of the huge closet attached to her bedroom. We're at the Bridgeport house, and I've just finished dressing for the party. I feel ridiculous wearing three-inch heels to a party being hosted on a lawn, but they are Louboutin's, making it impossible to resist when Gabby insisted I wear them.

I freeze in place, my eyes flying wide. "What? What's wrong?"

She glides over, walks in a wide circle around me, then stops in front of me. "You look absolutely stunning." She shakes her head. "No, not stunning. Sexy as sin!"

I feel my cheeks heat in response and brush my hands nervously down the skirt of my dress. It's Chanel, the one she thought would be perfect for me. The material is just a shade darker than the color of my skin and almost entirely made of chiffon, so it's soft and flowy. The skirt is layered and lands just above my knee. It has a corset style waist that sweeps up into a halter top, leaving most of my upper back exposed. "It's not too much for the party?"

"It's perfect!" She reaches out, clutching onto each of my upper arms, then leans forward to place a kiss on my cheek. "Seriously, I've never seen you look more radiant. This dress suits you."

I beam at her and then swirl around like a ballerina, a silly joy filling me as the skirt twirls up and around me. When I stop, the world around me continues to spin for a moment and I laugh out loud. "This is going to be fun!"

"See!" Gabby grabs my hand and pulls me out the door. "I told you! All we needed to do is dress you up and get you out of the city for a couple days!"

"You look amazing, too." I grin over at her. "In case I didn't tell you." She really does. She's wearing a red, strapless dress that's fitted on top but then flows down and flares out into a loose skirt right below her waist. And it's in the red that I refused to wear. It fits her perfectly.

"Well, thank you, darling," she drawls out in a haughty voice, giggling afterwards. "Let's hope I can find someone here that wants to take me out of it later."

My mouth falls momentarily open before I swat her playfully on the arm. "You are too much, Gabs! Your father is here somewhere! Don't you have any shame?"

"What Daddy doesn't know won't hurt him." She grins wickedly at me. "But, first, let's see if we can find a handsome someone for you. Let B.O.B have a little respite for the evening." Her brow rises as she smirks over at me.

Instead of my usual chastising, I merely roll my eyes and giggle along with her as we make our way down through the grand house and out onto the back lawn where the party is being held. Okay, I'm not sure if it's fair to call it a lawn. It's more like a small park, with long, rolling spans of green grass perfection stretching out to meet the rock wall that separates the yard from the water. It's truly a sight to behold, with sailboats moored and bobbing in the water beyond, brightened by the late afternoon sun shining on the soft waves.

There's a huge, white tent set up in the very middle of the

lawn, with beautifully decorated tables scattered throughout underneath. A wooden floor has been set up under the tent, as well as pathways over the entire lawn, making it easier for people to walk from here to there. I can hear music playing softly and know that there's probably a band somewhere under the tent, and wonder for a moment if there will be dancing later. There are people milling around throughout, many holding wine and champagne glasses, all looking relaxed and happy.

"Come on." Gabby grabs my hand and starts down one of the wood-laid paths. "Let's go find the bar!"

We are about to enter the tented area, when Gabby veers to the left and heads in another direction. "Let's go to that one." She points to a bar set up closer to the water. I nod my head in approval, always happy to be closer to the gorgeous view. When we arrive, she saunters past everyone standing in line and moves to the head of the bar.

"Gabby!" I whisper through clenched teeth, pulling at her hand. "There's a line!"

She looks over her shoulder at the line and smiles broadly at everyone before addressing them. "Daddy needs a drink pronto. No one minds, right?"

I roll my eyes at her brazen behavior and complete abuse of her 'daddy' privilege, but smile sweetly when she hands me a glass of champagne twenty seconds later. "You are such a spoiled, little brat when you want to be!"

"Hey, I can't use it for much, but when I can, I'm using it for all it's worth!" She clinks her glass against mine, laughing as we both take a sip of the bubbly liquid. It's cool, sweet, and so delicious as it slides past my lips and down my throat. *Okay, who am I to complain?*

"Did I hear someone say they were getting me a drink?" A deep voice sounds behind us, both of our eyes widening as our gazes lock before we spin around and smile brightly.

"Daddy!" Gabby steps forward and wraps her free arm around her father in a tight hug.

"How are you, my angel?" He hugs her with two hands, kissing her forehead as they release each other, a chuckle escaping him. "Not getting into trouble already, are you?"

"Of course not!" She takes a step back and motions to me. "You remember my friend Charlotte, right?"

He smiles at me and then leans forward, brushing a light kiss against my cheek. "Of course I do. And I also remember you like to be called Charlie, right?"

"I do." I return his smile and nod my head. "It's so nice to see you again, Mr. Reed. Thank you for letting me come to the party with Gabby."

He waves his hand. "Please, call me Ken. Mr. Reed makes me feel old!" His focus moves back to Gabby. "It's always nice to see Gabrielle with her friends."

"Where's Mother?" Gabby takes a sip of her champagne.

"Oh, she's here somewhere. I'm sure she's chatting up some guest for another donation." He laughs out loud and then sighs. "I suppose I should probably go do the same." He moves forward and kisses Gabby on the cheek. "Come sit with us at dinner if you wouldn't mind. I miss you."

"Okay, Daddy." She gives his arm a squeeze as he walks away. "I'll find you later." She turns her attention back to me and smiles, her cheeks flushing a little. "Sorry."

"What?" I tilt my head in surprise. "Why?"

"You know, because of your dad." She bites her bottom lip and blinks quickly. "I just didn't want to make you sad."

I squeeze my eyes shut for only a second, remembering my dad's funeral, only three months earlier, after a hard battle with cancer, then flutter them open, forcing a smile on my face. "It's okay. It actually didn't make me sad at all. It's nice to see you with your dad."

"But when he said he missed me, and I'm sure you miss your

dad, and you don't get to see him anymore, and it's just so unfair, and I'm sorry." Her words come out fast and she follows them up with another long gulp of champagne.

I smile and pull her into a hug. "I love you for thinking of me, but really, I'm okay." I release her and then take my own long drink, finishing off the last of my champagne. I hold the glass up and in attempt to lighten the mood call out, "Oh, bartender, Daddy needs another drink!" We burst out laughing, me in relief to move past the moment, and move back down the walkway toward the bar.

We spend the next hour mingling before finding and joining her parents for dinner at their table. The meal is delicious and filled with laughter and good company. After dessert is served, I excuse myself and make my way to the main house to use the bathroom and freshen up. After, I head back to the tent and attempt to find Gabby, but people are up and mingling, and dancing has begun, so I give up and go to the bar. I order a champagne. I've lost count how many I've consumed, but I feel happy and light so don't care. Taking my drink, I wander over to the edge of the dance floor to see if I can spot my little red siren of a friend.

The band is really good. They've been playing a wonderful mix of classics that has the dance floor filled with people, song after song. I smile when they begin to play "Moonlight in Vermont" and can't help myself as I begin swaying to the rhythm, remembering it as one of my mom and dad's favorite songs to dance to when I was little.

I'm startled out of my own thoughts when a voice behind me whispers, "Would you like to dance?" I turn toward the husky sound that just swept lightly over my ears and feel my heart miss a beat when my eyes land on the man before me.

CHAPTER FIVE

~Trey~

I have to keep myself from taking a step backwards as she turns to look at me, her eyes taking my breath away. When I saw her from across the bar a couple weeks ago, I swore they were lighter. Now that I'm staring into them, I can see that they aren't light at all. They are a solid walnut color, the outside rim surrounded completely by a thin darker ring. Yet, as dark as they may be, there is a softness to them I can't explain.

She blinks as I continue to absorb every detail of her face, her eyes changing from wide-eyed to curious in a matter of a second. "You're asking me to dance?"

"Yes." I nod my head and, in the same motion, take her champagne flute, set it on a nearby table, then place my hand against her lower back and guide her toward the floor. "I'm insisting."

"Oh!" Her feet move in approval even though I can tell from the myriad of expressions crossing her features that her head hasn't caught up. I put the slightest amount of pressure on her back, forcing her to turn into me, then curl my other hand around her fingers, pulling her flush to my body and begin to sway. In less than one turn, I feel her body relax, her delicate hand moving inside mine to lay flat. I look down and almost lose my step when my eyes lock onto hers again.

"I'm sorry. I saw you standing there, and you were moving to the music. You look so beautiful in this dress. I couldn't let all that be wasted." I offer her a small smile to go with my half-apology.

"It was my parents' favorite song to dance to." Her voice is tender, shy, and sentimental as her lips turn up just slightly as she holds my stare.

I can sense a sadness there and can't help myself from pressing for more. "Was?"

She finally breaks the hold her gaze has on me, blinking rapidly as she turns her head away. "My dad passed away several months ago." Her eyes snap back to mine, and with a small shrug, she continues. "No more "Moonlight in Vermont" for him."

"I'm sorry." I still my feet then, pausing the dance between us. "Do you want to stop?"

This time, it's she who forces my hand and pushes against me to keep moving. "No." She shakes her head, tilting it up to look at me, the corners of her mouth lifting into a gentle smile. "Let's keep dancing so I'll have a new memory to go with this song."

Holy shit. I'm the one that's supposed to be seducing her, but I think I'm the one that's in trouble here. I smile and nod, pulling her a fraction closer as I sway with her to the music. "I'm Maddox."

"Charlie." Her name is heat as it leaves her mouth and falls against the fabric of my shirt, her lips so close to my skin as her head rests against my chest. She's tiny in my arms. She's wearing heels and barely hits the top of my shoulder. I don't remember her looking this small when I saw her at the bar that night.

The song ends, but another immediately starts, and she makes no move to leave my arms, so I continue to hold her. Not another word is spoken between us as we move with each other, our bodies reacting to the rhythm of the music naturally, as if we'd danced together a hundred times. She's moved closer to me, my hand skating further up her back, fingertips gliding onto her bare skin, goosebumps erupting as I do. I pull back slightly and peek down at her. "Are you cold?"

She shakes her head, but instead of continuing our dance, she pulls away from me. "Do you want to get a drink?"

Fuck yes. "Sure." I remember what Trick said about letting her think she's the one in control here, and that she's seducing me, not the other way around and realize that's not going to be a problem at all. I try to rein in my controlling nature and follow behind her but know I'm losing when I see the skin of her bare back in front of me and instinctively put my hand there to guide her to the bar.

"So, Charlie's an unusual name for a girl. Is it a family name?" I'm curious and want to get to know her better. Although, I'm not sure it really matters, since this is a job and I'm just walking away in a few hours. I clench my jaw, cursing to myself in frustration.

Her cheeks turn a light pink as I catch her staring at me, her head whipping forward quickly when I try to make eye contact. "Oh, yeah, my name is actually Charlotte, but I've been Charlie for as long as I can remember."

We're in line at the bar now and she turns to glance up at me again, her forehead scrunching up as she does. "Have we met before? I feel like I've seen you somewhere. Maybe at another one of the Reed's functions?"

Shit! I guess she got a better look at me that night at the bar than I thought. "Nope, my first Reed event, and I definitely would remember if I'd met you before." I flash her one of my most charming smiles and begin to sweat.

"Charlie!" A high-pitched squeal comes at us from the side. "There you are!" A second later, a tangle of long, black hair and swishing red fabric is wrapped around Charlie. "I've been looking everywhere for you!"

"Hey!" They hug for a second and then break apart. "I've been right here. Where the heck have you been?" Charlie's brows raise high as she questions her friend, and I finally understand why

Trick wanted me to do this favor for him. I met her briefly at the bar, but didn't really pay much attention, writing her off as another one of Trick's conquests. But seeing her again, all long limbs, long hair, and I'm quite sure, long on other things that Trick likes, everything clicks.

"Ugh! Mother was dragging me all over the back lawn to speak to donors. I finally got away."

Charlie shifts and nods her head toward me but speaks to Gabby. "I was dancing with Maddox."

Gabby turns, is about to speak, but then stops, her mouth forming a very large, knowing smile. She, of course, knows who I am and instantly recognizes me from the bar. Her eyes scan me from head to toe before she finally extends a hand toward me. "Well, hello, Maddox. I'm Gabby."

I slide her hand into mine and give it a gentle squeeze before letting go. "Nice to meet you, Gabby."

Her brows raise for just an instant as she continues her obvious perusal of my frame before turning her attention back to Charlie. "I just wanted to tell you that Jake is going to take me out on his boat for a quick spin. I was going to ask you to go, but," she turns to look at me and then back at Charlie, "it looks like you're good here."

I watch as Charlie's cheeks turn a light pink again and find myself wondering what else on her body might turn that color under the right circumstances. As much as I didn't want to do this date for Trick, now that I've spent even just a few minutes with Charlie, I know I want a few more.

"Oh, no… It's not like that!" Charlie defends. "We were just getting something to drink. I don't want to hold Maddox up if he has something else to do."

Only you, baby. Only you. I smile and shake my head. "Nope. I'd love to get that drink and maybe another dance with you."

Gabby responds before Charlie even has a chance. "Perfect!" She then pulls Charlie by the arm and speaks in a lower voice.

"You are not saying no to Mr. Tie Me Up, Take Me Hard over there! Besides, I wasn't inviting you! I'm hoping to get more than a boat ride out of Jake, if you know what I mean."

I pretend I can't hear their conversation as I step up to the bar and order a glass of champagne for Charlie and a whiskey neat for myself, but listen as they continue to talk.

"Gabby, you are terrible!" Charlie says and giggles.

"Well, keep working that hunk of beef over there and you can be as terrible as me!"

"Shut up!" I hear a light slap. "He's going to hear you!"

"Good, you need to get laid!" Gabby giggles some more. "But, listen, would you mind staying in the guest cottage? I'm pretty sure things with Jake will take all night, if you know what I mean."

"Uh, yeah, of course. Will your parents mind?" Charlie asks.

"No, they probably won't even notice. The code is 7777 on the door lock." Gabby lets out a short, loud laugh. "I know, top secret, right?"

"Yeah. I feel super safe now." Charlie laughs back.

"Okay, I'm going to tell one of the staff to bring your suitcase down to the cottage. And I'll come find you in the morning, or you come find me, okay?"

"Sounds good."

I turn my head and watch as Gabby gives Charlie a quick hug, whispers something in her ear that makes her face turn a bright red, and then waves goodbye as she scurries off. To Jake and his boat, I assume. I walk over and hand the glass of champagne to her, which she takes. "You okay?"

She nods her head and smiles. "Yeah, yeah, of course. This is pretty typical. I love her like a sister but she's definitely a wild thing."

"Not you though?" I quip jokingly, bumping her shoulder lightly with my arm.

"Me?" Her eyes grow wide. "God no! She takes it to a whole new level. She tells me that any man she's remotely interested in gets an audition and that whether they get a call back is entirely up to them." She looks up at me and shakes her head, laughing. "I do not even want to know what the audition involves."

"So, what about me? Good enough for an audition?" I lock my eyes with hers, hoping she understands what I'm offering, at least the possibility of it, and keep staring until she finally looks away, drawing her lower lip between her teeth as she does.

~Charlotte~

oly shit! Is he saying what I think he's saying? I feel my face heating, again, and want to die from embarrassment. *Why does my body have to display my every reaction so blatantly?* "Why don't we just try another dance for now?"

His mouth curves up into a confident smile as he nods and then moves us in the direction of the dance floor. Fingers graze against my bare flesh as his hand lands gently on my upper back, goosebumps exploding across my skin, causing me to curse my damn body again. I take a fortifying gulp of my champagne for courage and step closer to him as we walk, instead of pulling away. I know I've sworn off men, but maybe, just once, I'll throw caution to the wind and live in the moment. I'll let myself have a little bit of much needed fun and not take any of what happens in the next few hours seriously. Because, Jesus, I really do need to get laid.

He responds by sliding his hand further around me, settling me into the crook of his arm. "Are you getting cold?" I can smell the whiskey on his breath as he leans down to speak to me, so close now.

I turn my head and lock my eyes onto his. "No."

One corner of his mouth cocks up as he holds my stare, his fingers sliding down my side, gripping lightly when they reach my hip. He guides me toward the dance floor, setting his drink and then mine on a table as we pass, never loosening his hold on me. When we're a quarter of the way through the couples already dancing, he turns and pulls my hip, yanking my body up against his, my arms wrapping instinctively around his neck.

"Oh," is all I can manage to utter as his other hand splays between my shoulders and presses my chest against his, my head coming to rest naturally below his chin. "Oh…" I say again, this time in pleasure, as the heat of him surrounds me and I feel the strength in his arms.

"Hmmm." He hums above me, the vibration in his throat tickling my forehead. "This is nice."

I bob my head in agreement, one hand sliding up the back of his neck until my fingers graze against the soft fuzz of his hair. It's cropped closely around the bottom but a bit longer on top, it's sandy color lighter than his chocolate-hued eyes. I inhale and close my eyes as I try to identify the scent that floats from him. It reminds me of the air in the fall when crisp leaves are swept up in the wind and swirl around you, fresh and light but hinted with musk.

"So, Maddox, what brings you to the Reed's tonight?" I try and make conversation to keep this moment lighter than the direction it seems to be going in.

I feel his head shake back and forth, and his chest vibrates against my cheek as he speaks. "Same thing as you I suppose. I'm here for a friend."

"Oh, would I know him? Is he a friend of Gabby's?"

"I'm sure it's something like that." His hand shifts on my hip and angles my body so it's more aligned with his, and I gasp slightly when I feel his length press against me. I'm not sure it's hard, but it's definitely impossible to miss and turns me mute as a wave of desire sweeps over me.

With each turn, we move a fraction closer to each other until I don't think there is a single breadth of space between us. His hand has moved from my hip to the top of my buttocks, while the other remains pressed wide and flat on the bare skin below my neck. I'm hot in so many places, but the heat pulsing below my waist is slowly building to an inferno the longer we stay on this dance floor. I've lost count of how many songs we've rocked back and forth to but it's enough to know I'm close to my breaking point.

As if he can read my thoughts, his hot breath is suddenly at my ear. "Want to take a walk? Cool off?"

I turn my head to the sound of his voice and freeze when my lips almost collide against his. My eyes trail in a slow line up the smooth plains of his face and latch onto his very dark, very intense pupils. His hand drifts up my back, my shoulder, and then my neck before coming to rest on my cheek. His thumb sweeps gently over my bottom lip, his gaze shifting lower as my mouth opens a fraction wider and my tongue darts out to wet my upper lip.

A long, hot breath leaves him and mingles with mine, his eyes closing for a brief moment before opening on a low growl. "I'm trying to be a gentleman here, Charlotte, but if you keep looking at me like that, I'm not sure how much longer that's going to last."

I blink once, breaking the spell I seem to be under, and then lean forward, closing my eyes as I press my lips against his. His fingers tighten the smallest bit against my face as he seems to fight some kind of internal battle and then relax as they slide around the nape of my neck, pulling me closer to deepen the kiss.

Searing heat spears through my body the moment my mouth meets his, my grip on him tightening as tingles travel to the very tips of my toes, throwing me off balance. I groan, which he uses to his advantage, intensifying the kiss, swirling his tongue around mine, our breaths becoming one. My hand becomes a fist, clenching onto the material of his shirt, bunching it into a tight ball to keep myself from falling.

And then his lips are gone, and just as quickly, I realize what I just did. My eyes fly up to meet his, even darker now, both of us breathing hard. "I'm sorry. I don't know why I did that."

"Don't be." His reply husky. "I'm glad you did." His thumb swipes against my bottom lip, pulling it gently out of my teeth, then he leans forward, brushing a light kiss against it. "Come."

He releases my face to take my hand, leading me off of the dance floor and then down one of the wooden paths to the stone wall overlooking the ocean. He pulls my hand, steering me off the path and onto the grass, walking parallel with the wall until we are no longer visible to the party. I can't believe I'm letting him lead me into a dark corner, away from everyone. He's just shy of a being a complete stranger. But, for some reason, it doesn't feel wrong. *He* doesn't feel wrong. Maybe it's the champagne. Or the dancing. Or the fact I haven't had sex with a man in three months. Right now, I just don't care.

He stops and leans against the wall, his ass the perfect height to rest against it comfortably, and then tugs me between his legs. My hands slide over the soft material of his dress pants along his thighs and come to rest at his waist. I rest my head against his chest, letting out a sigh. His lips press against the top of my head as he wraps his arms around me and pulls me closer.

"Are you okay?" His question is a bit muffled as his lips move against my locks.

I nod my head but stay hidden against his chest. "I don't do things like this." I feel a chuckle rumble in his chest and finally look up. "I don't."

He smiles down at me. "I believe you." He arches a brow and looks around. "I'm just not sure that we've done anything."

"Yet," I finish.

"Yet implies that you think something will happen or that you want it to."

"Don't you?" I reply quickly, not thinking of what I'm asking. I only know that I want to know that he feels the same way.

His hand leaves my waist and glides up the flat plane of my stomach, through the valley between my breasts and then up my neck until his fingers raise my chin, forcing my eyes to his. "More than you can imagine."

My heart is thundering in my chest as I whisper my next words. "Then kiss me again. Kiss me like you've been in the desert for a month and I'm a glass of water."

"Jesus Christ, Charlotte." His hand snakes through my hair as he yanks me up to his mouth. "I'm fucking parched," is all I hear before his lips are on mine. And they are burning hot, like I imagine the sands of the Sahara would be.

CHAPTER SIX

~Trey~

After several long minutes, I tear my lips from hers to a
moan of protest, one tiny hand fisted in my shirt, the other
grasping onto the back of my head. "Why are you stopping?"

Because I'm about to come in my fucking pants. "Didn't I hear
Gabby say something about a guest house?" I pant out, planting a
kiss against her forehead as I stand, her body warm and pliant
against mine, her grip on me relaxing. *And, shit, I know I'm only
supposed to woo her, but there is no way I'm stopping now.*

"Oh, yes!" She runs her fingers through her now tousled hair
and takes a step away from me to point in the direction of the
house. "It's on the other side of the pool. I'm staying there
tonight."

You mean, we're *staying there tonight.* "Should we go there?
Probably more comfortable than this wall?" I rise and grasp her
hand in mine when she nods yes, starting towards the direction
she pointed. "Lead the way."

We follow the wooden path back to the main house and then
veer to the left around the pool, and just as she said, a small house

comes into view. I follow her up onto the porch and watch as she punches in the code on the lock, pushing the door open when the light turns green. She steps through and flips on a switch, illuminating the living area we're now standing in. She turns to look at me and smiles shyly. "I'll be right back. There's probably stuff to drink in the fridge if you want to check."

"Okay, sure." I nod as she turns and heads across the living room into a bathroom, shutting the door behind her. I spin on my heel, looking around the place, and see a kitchen through another doorway. As I walk in that direction, I notice a small wet bar in the dining room so make a detour there instead. I grin broadly when I find a bottle of good whiskey and quickly pour myself a glass.

I frown because I have no idea what Charlotte likes, besides champagne, and find that I don't like not knowing. I usually go into an arrangement knowing what a client likes and doesn't. But then, I guess she isn't my typical client. I stroll back the way I came and stand in front of the bathroom door. "Do you like whiskey?"

"Not particularly," she calls from the other side. "Tequila works."

My brows rise in surprise. Well, shit. That's not an answer I would have expected. She keeps breaking the mold I made up of her in my mind. I need to stop doing that. I go and fetch the requested drink and find her standing in the living room when I return.

She's taken her shoes off, and I can't help but think how she looks even more tiny to me now. She's like a little pixie but with the heart of a minx. I hand her the tumbler of Patron I've poured and clink my glass against hers. "Cheers."

Surprising me again, she raises the glass to her mouth and swallows the entire glass in two gulps. "Holy shit, Charlotte! That's a lot of tequila!"

She smiles sweetly. "I'm a big girl, Maddox, don't worry." Her voice has dropped an octave, making it almost raspy, and it shoots straight to my dick. *What the fuck is this girl doing to me?* I literally cannot remember the last time I *wanted* to be with someone instead of *having* to be with them. And I know I shouldn't be doing this. This definitely isn't part of the job. But this girl, everything about her has me acting on instinct, not off some instructions Trick gave.

She swishes by me in her dress to switch on a lamp and then flicks the overhead light switch off. The mood of the room changes immediately, now bathed in a soft yellow glow. She twirls back around and tilts her head. "Why do you keep calling me Charlotte? Everyone calls me Charlie."

I down the rest of my whiskey in a single swallow and move around her to set my glass on the table. I turn and walk so she's standing in front of me. "Come here." I crook my finger and motion for her to come closer.

She doesn't hesitate and moves instantly, pressing her body against mine, wrapping her arms around me. "Because, I'm not like everyone else." I gather her face in my hands and cover her mouth with mine. Her lips open immediately, her tongue snaking out to find mine. I feel her hands move to the front of my chest and then her fingers as they begin to work the buttons on my shirt. I release her face and reach down to pull the bottom half of my shirt out of my pants and then break away as I pull the shirt over my head.

"Wow." Her eyes are wide as she steps back from me, trapping her bottom lip between her teeth, and places both hands on my chest. Her eyes trail over my torso and then down my stomach, her fingers soon following, tracing the lines of my muscles as she explores. When she reaches my waist, her eyes skim back up to meet mine, and she shakes her head. "You're gorgeous."

You're gorgeous. I chuckle and then pull her hand to my mouth and place a kiss on her palm. "It's your turn."

"My turn?" She stammers.

"Take the dress off." *Before I rip it off.*

She takes her other hand off my waist and takes a small step back. She skims a hand up her side, moving it under her arm and then grasps onto a zipper and lowers it. When it's all the way down, she turns so that her back faces me, raising her arms to her neck to untie the knot holding up the top portion of the dress. When both pieces are free, she moves the fabric away from her shoulders and then releases them, the entire dress sliding down her body in one swish.

She's standing before me in only a nude pair of lace panties, her back to me, and I'm already so fucking hard that I don't know how my dick is going to stay in my pants when she turns around. But there's no way I'm stopping now. "Turn around."

And she does. In one swift motion, and in less than a second, she rotates and my heart fucking stops in my chest. She's perfection. Before I can truly take her in, she takes three bold steps toward me, lays her hand flat against my chest, and pushes me until the back of my legs hit the couch. She shoves me hard enough so that I sit, and before I can even blink, she's straddled my lap. Her arms snake around my neck, her fingers landing in my hair, her forehead bumping against mine. Hot air flutters out between her lips as she exhales and then whispers, "I'm sorry."

I'm not. "For what?" I reach up and stroke the loose strands of hair against her face away, holding her head in my hands.

"Because I said I don't do this." Her tongue darts out and slides across her bottom lip, leaving it wet and shiny and my resolve on thin ice.

Oh, we're so doing this. "Do you want to stop?" I skim one hand gently across her face and trace the wet trail along her bottom lip with my thumb, my eyes staying locked on hers. She shakes her head, sucking the tip of my thumb into the heat of her mouth at the same time, eliciting a chuckle from me. "I'll take that as a no." I pop my thumb from her hold and crash my lips to hers, sweeping my tongue against them, forcing her to open. I can taste the tequila on her and delve deeper as her arms tighten around me and her fingers clench and pull my short hair. My cock throbs as her hardened nipples brush against my own, and I move my hand down to push her core down as I rock into it.

Her mouth parts as it falls open in a moan, her eyes shooting up to meet mine. She shifts her ass back, my brows furrowing in question, until she leans forward and begins a slow assault with her lips down my neck. She continues to move lower, sliding her body off my legs as she does, bracing her hands on my chest as her tongue grazes down my pec and swirls around one of my nipples. Her eyes peek up at me from under heavy lashes as she drags it over the peak and then closes her lips around the raised disk and sucks. "Fuck me..." I groan out, my eyes snapping shut as my cock throbs in agony.

I feel her lips form a smile right before cold air hits my wet nipple and almost come when I hear her respond. "I'm getting there." *Fuuuck.*

I move to sit up, but her hands slap against my chest, pushing me back, her head shaking back and forth. "I'm not done yet."

Holy fucking hell. I'm in so much trouble. I chuckle and submit, relaxing back into the couch as her tiny fingers scrape down my chest until they reach my waistband, making quick work of the buckle on my belt. Next, I feel her release the hook on my pants and then lower the zipper, another moan escaping me as some of the pressure on my pounding cock is finally relieved. Her hands grasp the fabric on both sides of my hips and begin pulling, so I raise my ass and move to help her push them off my waist and down my legs.

She scoots back to pull them completely off and then places a hand on each of my thighs as she settles herself back between my legs. Her eyes are fixed on my hard length, jutting up against my lower abdomen. I watch as her fingers skim up my thigh until they reach to wrap around my shaft and then squeeze. "You're so big."

All the better to fuck you with. "Only because your hands are so damn small." I cover her hand with mine and guide her to stroke up and down before the grip she has on my cock makes me explode. She bends forward at the same time and hot, wet heat trails up the head of my cock as her tongue slides over it. I groan, releasing the hold on her hand, my head falling back as she continues licking me, until she finally wraps her lips around my crown and sucks me deep into her mouth.

I hiss and latch my hands around her head as my dick hits the back of her throat and she swallows. "Sweet Jesus, Charlotte." She slides back until I think I'm about to pop out of her mouth and then sucks again, drawing me all the way back in. I push my feet into the floor, bracing myself from surging my hips forward like I want. I want to fuck her face so goddamn bad, but I'm trying to let her control this moment. She bobs her head several more times, her hair brushing against my thighs every time her lips meet my groin, until I can't take another second.

"I'm going to fucking explode in your mouth, and I'm not done with you yet," I growl out as I tighten my grip around her head and pull her all the way off my cock, a soft yelp escaping as she looks up at me. "Hand me my pants."

She twists, reaching for them, and then hands them to me. I turn them around until I find the pockets and then dig around until I find what I'm looking for. I drop the pants and place one corner of the foil packet in my mouth and then pull, tearing it open. Realizing what I'm doing, she grabs it and pulls out the condom, moving to stand over me.

~Charlotte~

I *can't believe I'm doing this. I'm going to have sex with a total stranger. I don't even know his last name.* I roll the condom down and look back up at him. He's fucking gorgeous. I don't even care if I don't know his last name. I must have hesitated for too long because his eyes have narrowed and his hands have stilled on my hips.

"Are you sure you want to do this?" His eyes have softened around the edges, and the dark, lustful look that invaded them just seconds ago has evaporated.

"I'm sure." I nod as if this will provide further proof of my willingness. He doesn't need it. The second my words reach his ears, his grip on my waist tightens to pull me onto his lap.

"Then kiss me, 'cause I'm still thirsty." And then his lips are crashing against mine, his tongue forcing my mouth open as he plunges inside. I surge into him, his cock hard and jutting against my clit. I moan against his mouth, the pure ecstasy that one contact against my starving pussy elicits, and rub again.

His lips curve up at my response and then move away from mine. "Are you ready?" He slides a hand between us and positions himself under me. I bump my forehead against his as I nod, lowering myself on top of him.

My mouth falls open in a silent cry as I sink down, his length slowly sliding in. *It wasn't my hands; he's huge!* I can feel myself spreading around his girth and pulse around it as my clit feels every inch going in.

"Jesus, so fucking tight." Maddox's fingers are digging into my hip on one side, while the others are locked around my neck as he stares into my eyes. "You okay?"

"Uh-huh." I nod furiously and then clench my eyes closed as I begin to wonder if he's going to fit all the way in.

"Shhhh, relax," he breathes out as I feel his lips against my neck. He nips a trail down my chest, stopping when he finds one of my breasts. He pulls my taut bud into his mouth and flicks his tongue before sucking hard, my hips thrusting involuntarily, driving his cock all the way home.

"Ohhhh!" I clench around him, my nails digging into the back of his arms, his lips sucking harder on my peak, my body rocking against him again. He laves his tongue one last time over my nipple and then lifts his head, sealing his lips over mine. I feel my body relax and melt into him. I slowly begin to ease my pussy up and down his length. It's been months since I've been with anyone, and I can already feel my body start to react and quicken, even though he's only been inside me for a minute.

"Jesus, you feel so fucking good," he murmurs against my mouth, his grip clenching more tightly as he plunges his cock deeper into me.

"So good," I manage to pant out and spread my legs wider, driving myself deeper and harder against him, sweat breaking across my skin in a thin sheen. "Don't stop. Please don't stop," I hear myself beg, clutching onto him wildly as I increase my bucking, my clit beginning to throb. "I'm going to come!"

His hand splays across my ass and he pushes hard, driving his cock deep, ripping my orgasm from me. "Yes! Yes! Yes!" I wrap myself around him, clinging tightly, ripples of electricity surging through my body. He continues pumping slowly into me, drawing out every ounce of pleasure, his lips kissing mine hungrily. "That—was—so—"

"We're not done yet," he growls as he pulls me off him and stands. His hand is in my hair as he pulls me roughly up against him, smashing my mouth back against his, ravaging it with his tongue. He pulls away after a moment, panting, eyes blazing. "Still fucking thirsty."

My pulse quickens at the desire boiling over in him, and I realize I don't want him to be done with me yet. "Okay." I slide my hands up his delicious torso and press my lips against his chest. I could spend the next hour tracing every groove lining his stomach and die a happy woman.

"Is there a bed?" He slides a finger under my chin to lift it. "Somewhere I can fuck you properly?"

Oh. My. God. I think I just came again. "Of course," I manage to splutter out. "It's that way." I point in the direction of the bedroom and he takes my hand, leading the way.

When we reach the door, he pushes it open, turning at the same time, pulling me back into his arms, his lips finding mine again. I fling my arms back around his neck and hold on as he guides me to the bed and lowers me down. *This is too easy. He's too good at this. He's too perfect.* The same thoughts keep running through my head, but I don't want to stop. Can't stop now.

His lips have left mine and are trailing down my body, over my nipples, my stomach, and now linger at the apex of my thighs. "I'm going to kiss you here now." His voice vibrates between my legs. I feel a finger dip into my wet center at the same time his lips wrap around my clit and suck gently.

I grasp onto the bedding as my back arches off the bed. "Ohhh!" His hand reaches across my hip and pushes it flat against the bed again. He sucks again, pushing his finger all the way into me and I gasp in pleasure. I've never come twice before, but if he keeps doing this, I know I will.

"I'm gonna make you feel so good Charlotte. Better than you ever have before." He flicks his tongue back and forth over my clit as he plunges a second finger inside me and I believe him. Every. Fucking. Word.

"Yes," I mewl out. "Feels so good." I can hear my juices around his fingers as another orgasm begins to build, and I begin grinding my pussy up against his hand.

"You want more, baby?" He's leaning over me now, his lips a fraction from mine, the smell of me strong, his fingers still slamming into me.

"Yes! Please!" I lift my head and smash my mouth against his, sucking in my own taste, hungry for every little piece of him. I feel his fingers leave me and yell out when his cock slams inside of me to take their place.

"Sweet fucking Jesus. Already forgot how tight you are." He moans against my mouth as he plunges inside me. "Feels so fucking good."

I just nod my head, drowning in the sensation of the orgasm threatening to take me again. I cling to him desperately as he shifts his waist lower, raising my legs as he does, and hits a spot I've only heard about. It takes only two strokes until my entire body tightens around him like a vise, my fingernails ripping along his back, another orgasm rolling through me as I cry out.

"Fuck yes!" Maddox bellows, pumping into me hard two more times, his own release finally throbbing between my pussy. "Fucking perfect," he moans out as I feel the last few pulses tremble from him.

He lays over me for just a minute before gently pulling out of me to roll over onto his back, tugging me up against his side as he does. I can feel his heart thundering against his chest as he pants lightly. His skin is damp, even though I can feel heat radiating off him. "You okay?"

My nose tickles from the vibration of his chest, and I smile. "Better than okay. Are you okay?"

He chuckles and kisses the top of my head. "Definitely better than okay. You were amazing."

"I've never done that before," I whisper.

"What?" He moves to lean over me.

I hide my face under my hand in embarrassment and then spit out my confession. "Came twice in one night." I shake my head, still hiding behind my hand. "Maybe it was the tequila."

"Hey." His hand settles over mine to move it gently from my face. "It wasn't the tequila." And then his lips are on mine, kissing me softly before drawing away. "You've obviously been with all the wrong guys."

I grunt and laugh out loud. "You have no idea." I reach my hand out and place it on his cheek. "So, are you the right guy?"

I feel his entire body tighten and then just as quickly relax as he forces a tight smile. "I'm just a guy." He plants a quick kiss on my forehead and sits up abruptly. "I'm going to go clean up. Need anything?" Then he rises from the bed, his back already in the doorframe before I can reply.

CHAPTER SEVEN

~Trey~

F*uck! What the hell have I gotten myself into?* I knew seducing this girl would be easy, but who knew letting her go was going to be the hard part? She is fucking perfect. Everything about her. From her easy laugh, to her gorgeous chocolate eyes, to her surprisingly dominant, little sassy self she tries to hide. I stare at my reflection in the mirror and run a hand down my features, hoping to swipe away the confusion I'm feeling. It doesn't work.

I sigh and reach down to roll the condom off my dick that's still half erect from just thinking about her. I tie it in a knot, throw it in the toilet, and then flush it away after I relieve myself. I wash my hands, splashing cold water over my face a few times, knowing I'm stalling. This can't be anything more than what it is: my job.

Trick hired me to make this girl feel good for one night. So she could remember what it felt like to have a guy be good to her. And, damn it, I did that. I made her come twice. She begged me for it. My job is done. I scoff, knowing that I so crossed the line when it came to what this job was supposed to be. Because, how good is she going to fucking feel when I walk out that door and she never hears from me again? And why the hell does that bother me so much?

I avoid looking at myself in the mirror as I find a wash cloth and run it under hot water. I want to clean her up and hold her a while longer before I have leave. I wring it out and then walk back toward the bedroom. I take a deep breath, blowing out all the crap running through my head, and then push the door open wide. I freeze when my eyes land on the vision before me. She's curled on her side, hands resting under her cheek like an angel, eyes closed, her chest rising and falling as she sleeps. Her hair is tousled and laying loosely around her face like a soft frame. She's naked and I want so badly to slide behind her, slip my arms around her, and just hold her while she sleeps. But, I know if I do, it will be the start of something that I just can't allow with a client. Not that she's even aware that she's a client. That's what's so fucked up about this. If I'd met her as 'Trey' instead of as fucking Maddox, I'd already be in that bed with her.

I let out a tired breath and then leave, going back to the bathroom to return the wash cloth. I find a soft blanket in a big wicker basket in the living room and tread quietly back into the room to cover her. When she's completely wrapped, she curls into a tighter ball, mumbling incoherently before settling into a relaxed slumber again. I skim my fingers lightly over her locks and bend to place a soft kiss on her temple.

"Sweet dreams, Charlotte," I whisper and then turn and exit the room, shutting the door gently behind me. I gather my trail of clothes scattered across the living room and dress in silence as I recount my evening. It's one of the best I've had in a long time. It sucks that I finally met a girl I'd actually like to see again, and she's a fucking job. I hate that she's probably going to wake up in the morning and just think of me as another asshole who fucked her over. Literally.

I slide my shoes on and then walk to the kitchen and begin

opening drawers until I find what I'm looking for. I sit at the table and tap the pen against my forehead as I try to think of the correct words to write.

'sorry to chew and screw'

'job well done'

'sorry, not sorry?'

Obviously, none of that shit is going to work. I decide the best thing I can do is just to try and keep it simple and hope it's enough for her to know what happened was special. I read the words I wrote one more time and then quietly leave the cottage. It's only been an hour since I walked through the door, but it feels like something has shifted, making the world feel different to me as I make my way around the front of the house.

I pull my phone out of my pocket and call for an Uber, noting it's just after midnight. I get a message stating a driver is on the way and should be here in ten minutes. I bring up my contacts and hit Trick's number. It rings twice before he picks up.

"Did you redeem all men for us?" He sounds like he's panting.

"What the fuck are you doing? You sound like you're lifting weights."

"I'm at The Den." This is all he needs to say for me to under-stand what he's doing. The Den is an underground BDSM club that specializes in the kind of things you only read about in books.

"What the fuck did you answer for then?"

"Because, when you call, I fucking answer. Especially when you're doing a favor for me." I hear a loud thwack followed by a low moan and shudder. "So, why you calling? There a problem?"

"I fucked her." I blow out a long breath.

"And that's a problem?" The phone grows muffled for a moment, but I can still make out some of what he's saying to whomever he's with and I shake my head in disbelief.

"You there?" I grumble. "Trick, I'll just call you back."

"Nah, it's all good now. You'd be surprised how quickly one

shuts up when you wrap a—never mind. Who cares if you fucked her? Just means she got the bonus plan." I hear another thwack.

"I like her." I shrug, even though I know he can't see the action. He's silent long enough that I'm not sure if he heard me. "You still there?"

"Yeah." Another twenty seconds of silence. "It's a fucking job, man. It's done. Store it away. You don't ever have to see this chick again."

But I want to. "Yeah, I know. I just feel like shit sneaking out in the middle of the night." I sigh and drag my hand through my hair. "She's gorgeous. First girl in a long time to fucking ring my bell. You know what I'm saying?"

"You want your bell fucking rang? I'll take you here. She's a job. Feelings ain't allowed."

"You're a prick. Anyone ever tell you that?" I throw back at him. I know he's keeping it real for me, but right now, it isn't what I want to hear.

"Every fucking day, man." The phone clicks and it's silent. I pull it away from my ear to see if he hung up, and yep, asshole hung up on me. I shake my head again and laugh, because it just wouldn't be Trick if he didn't call it like it fucking was.

"Hey, handsome." I turn, my brows rising in surprise when I see Gabby strolling toward me.

"Hey yourself." I offer a small wave.

She stops in front of me, leans toward me inhaling, and then grins wickedly. "Oh!" Her brows rise. "You smell like sex. You take extra-care of my girl?"

Jesus, she and Trick are a fucking perfect pair. "She's sleeping. I just left her in the guest cottage."

"So you did fuck her? Trick said you wouldn't, that it went against your rules. He also said you're a god in the sack." She trails one finger down my chest until her hand reaches my waist and then slides it over my dick, cupping it roughly. "Certainly seem to have the goods."

Instead of backing away, I reach a hand up and grasp her around the throat and squeeze lightly, a surprised gasp sounding from her. "This what you like, Gabby?" I snort when she nods her head, her tongue slipping out to wet her lips. "You like to play games." I squeeze just a little harder. "Like it a little rough?"

She lets out a soft moan and then tightens the grip she has on my still soft cock. I release her throat, pushing her back at the same time, and then snicker. "Yeah, I gave it to her real good. You happy?" I step into her space then, so my mouth is just an inch from hers. "You better be there for her tomorrow when she wakes up, 'cause not everything's a fucking game."

She scoffs and clicks a red fingernail against her matching lips. "I'll give your money to Trick this week."

"Keep your money. I don't want it," I practically spit back at her.

Headlights sweep across the driveway as I step away from her again, her eyes narrowing as she keeps her gaze locked on me then smiles wide. "You like her."

The car comes to a stop next to me, the passenger window lowering as the driver leans over. "You call for an Uber?"

I nod. "Yep." I open the back door and turn back to Gabby. "Just make sure she's okay in the morning." Then I get in the car and slam the door before she has a chance to respond, an ear-splitting grin still plastered on her face as the car pulls away.

~Charlotte~

I'll never hear "Moonlight in Vermont" again without thinking of you. Hope our paths cross again. XO ~Maddox

I stare at the piece of paper with the two simple sentences he left behind and then drop it. It floats silently through the air before coming to rest next to my hand on the bed. My eyes lock onto the swirling blades of the ceiling fan above me, a real-life example of what my mind is doing right now. My fingers move blindly until they skim over the paper and grasp onto it. I raise it to my nose and inhale deeply, trying to see if I can find his scent.

He was everything I could have wanted in a one night stand. A perfect gentleman. And every decision made to sleep with him was mine. I left the dance floor, I followed him down to the water, I led him back to the cottage, and I knew exactly what I was getting myself into. And wow. Just thinking about him causes my pussy to throb. I've slept with enough guys to know that this one was different. This one was good. We were good. Why didn't he leave his number for me then?

Maybe he isn't from around here. I didn't even ask. I don't even know his last name. I've never slept with someone I've just met, let alone without knowing their complete name and address. I slap a hand over my face and groan out loud. "I'm such a slut."

"Now those are words I know well." Gabby bounces onto the bed next to me and holds out a covered cup of coffee. "Morning, you dirty whore."

"Takes one to know one, bitch," I respond smugly, as I gratefully grab the coffee from her and take a long sip. "Heaven. Thank you."

"Sure." Her eyes land on the now mostly crumpled piece of paper lying next to me, and before I can react, she swipes it and reads it. Her face lights up in a smirk as she looks over at me. "So, was it amazing? Tell me everything! He was smoking hot, by the way!"

With my free hand, I grab a throw pillow and hide my face under it as I moan out loud. "It was *so* good, Gabby!"

She pulls the pillow off my face and throws it on the floor. "So, why are you hiding under this thing? I want details! And stop with the blushing! You've done nothing wrong!"

"Gabs!" I exclaim, my voice going shrill in disbelief. "I had sex with a total stranger! I don't even know his last name! I don't even know where he's from!"

Her shoulders rise and fall. "So. That's the best kind, if you ask me. What's the big deal?"

One side of my mouth crooks up as I shrug. "I don't know. I just don't do that." I spread my hand flat over my face and peek out between my fingers. "But, Jesus, Gabby, you should have seen him naked. His chest was like a piece of damn chiseled art. And we see naked bodies all the time!"

"But did he know what to do with that body?" She cocks her head. "Because, man, what a waste that would be if he didn't."

I nod my head up and down vigorously. "Um, yeah. He definitely knew what he was doing." I sigh in delight at the memory. "I mean, oh my God, Gabs. He was *so* good."

"You *are* a little slut, aren't you!" She cackles and slaps me playfully on the leg. "We'll have to set you up on Tinder and get you swiping right! I'm telling you, casual-no-strings-sex is the way to go. No muss. No fuss."

"Ew! No thank you! This was a one-time thing!" I rise up out of the bed, stretching my sore-in-all-the-right-places body and grin widely. "I'll never be you, my friend."

I watch as she also stands, her eyebrows rising as the corners of her mouth turn-up into a confident smile. "Impossible to achieve this type of perfection."

I pick the pillow up off the floor and throw it at her teasingly. "Yes, impossible." She ducks and sticks her tongue out at me.

"You hungry?" she asks as I rifle through the overnight bag someone left by the side of the bed at some point. I pull a teal shirt out and slide it over my naked body then slip a pair of leggings on.

"I'm famished!" I bend over, digging through the bag again until I find my tooth brush, waving it in the air victoriously once I do. "But I have to brush my teeth. It feels like the Sahara Desert in my mouth." As I say the last sentence, his raspy voice echoes through my head in memory. *"I'm fucking parched."* And I skim my fingers over my lips, remembering the way his felt against mine.

"What?" Gabby's looking at me like I've grown an extra head. "What's that look on your face?"

I decide that some things about last night don't need to be shared and offer her a small smile instead as I glide past her and head to the bathroom. "Nothing."

"Ouoh, that ain't nothing, girl." She follows behind me. "You're hiding something."

I shake my head as I turn the faucet on and wet my toothbrush, squirting toothpaste on it before sticking it into my mouth. I grin around the brush, foam building around my lips, and shrug instead of answering again.

"I'll get it out of you." She waggles her finger in front of me. "One way or another, one bottle of wine or another."

I giggle around my brush and then turn back to the sink to finish my chore. When I'm done, I breeze back by her, humming, knowing my nonchalant act is driving her mad, to put my toothbrush away. "Did you say something about food?"

She shakes her head, one side of her mouth crooked up in a smile. "Come on, you dirty little thing. Let's go feed you."

CHAPTER EIGHT

~Trey~

"I think it's weird that you're going to see her again." Trick's sitting in his usual spot on the couch, beer in hand, as he watches me lace up my dress shoes.

"Why? I like her. She's great company." I straighten and grab my suit jacket off the back of the chair I left it on a few minutes ago.

"She's fucking old, man, that's why. It's kind of creepy." He takes a swig of his beer, a look a disgust on her face.

"I'm not sleeping with her, dude." I snort at his lack of depth and slide my jacket on over my white dress shirt. "She listens to me and offers great advice."

"I give you great advice, man," he counters, sitting up straight.

"Jesus, Trick." I chuckle. "It's not like I'm cheating on you. And you only give me advice on how to wet my dick. I got that covered."

"Whatever, asshole," he grumbles under his breath, shaking his head. "I still think it's weird."

"Well, I think it's strange that a thirty-year-old guy, with a professional pilot's license, sits here playing fucking video games all day flying fake fucking helicopters, when you could be out doing the real thing." It's a low blow, and I know it's going to hit a nerve, but I need something to light a fire under his ass and get him off this damn couch. Besides The Den.

His head swivels, dark green eyes burning in anger as they lock onto mine. He stands and throws his beer bottle against a wall, brown glass flying in shards around our kitchen. "Fuck you, Trey." He takes three longs strides to stand directly in front of me, so close I can smell the beer on his breath. Some people might be intimidated by him; his attitude, his muscular frame, the way hot breaths are blowing out his nostrils right now, but not me. I know way too much about him and what he would and wouldn't do.

"You wanna go there with me right now?" he huffs out.

I look down at him and scoff. "Got you off the couch, didn't I?"

He stares me down for a second before a sick kind of grin splays across his face as he takes a step back. "Fuck off. Get out of here before you're late for your *date*."

"Don't worry about me, asshole. Worry about yourself." I grab my keys out of dish by the door before pulling it open. "You better not skip your damn appointment tomorrow. You're on the edge, Patrick."

I don't wait for him to reply and slam the door behind me before I can hear a response that I'm sure will contain more than one expletive. I know I'm being a dick to him, but if he misses another appointment with his shrink, Cory's not going to let him work. I take the stairs down to meet my driver instead of the elevator to shake off my argument with Trick.

I exit my building and find Gene leaning against his car. As I approach, he shifts off the vehicle and moves to open the back door for me. "How ya doing tonight, sir?" I've never asked, but I'm pretty sure he's from Brooklyn with that heavy New York accent.

"You can call me Trey." It feels strange as hell when someone thirty years older than me calls me sir. "I've told you at least twenty times."

"Yes, sir," is all I get as he shuts the door after me. He climbs into the driver's seat a few seconds later and winks at me in the rear view. "Mrs. Perry's residence?"

"Actually, no. She's meeting me at the restaurant. She was out doing some shopping and called to say it was easier for her to just stay out."

"Very good, sir."

I meet his twinkling eyes in the rear view and raise my brow in disbelief. He's never going to change, so I don't know why I bother. Twenty minutes later, we pull up outside of the Polo Bar in mid-town where a valet has my door open in seconds. "Gene, I'll call when we're done. Probably two hours."

"Yes, sir."

I shake my head as I step out of the car and then stride through the door into the restaurant. I'm ten minutes early, but if she isn't already here, I'd be shocked. It's the third time I've met with her since the original event she hired me for, and she's early every time. I'm not on the clock anymore. I meet with her because she fascinates me. She insists on paying every time we're together, touting her ability to do so as an excuse, and, because it seems to give her pleasure, I haven't argued.

I approach the hostess' station and let them know I have a reservation for two under Perry. Yes, we used her name. The Polo Bar caters to the wealthy, and if you aren't on a list they like, you aren't getting a table here. The pretty blonde behind the podium nods her head at me and motions for me to follow. "Of course, your party is already here. Right this way."

I've been to the restaurant once before and immediately remember its unique equestrian feel as I'm led to the table. Everything is soft, brown leather and trimmed in supple hunter green. It reminds me of stepping back in time or of how I think a fine restaurant in the English countryside might look. Horse paintings line the richly painted walls, making it feel like eyes are following me as I pass through the room.

I'm relieved when I see Karen and smile in greeting as I approach. "Don't get up." I move to the leather bench she's sitting on and bend to place a kiss on her cheek. "You look lovely as always."

She laughs lightly and waves a hand in dismissal. "And you're just as charming as ever."

I sit in the seat across from her and reach my hand across the table to give hers a gentle squeeze. "Really, you look great today. What has you so happy?"

A smile graces her thin but still pretty lips as her eyes roam over the room around us. "I used to come here with Astor all the time. It was one of his favorite places to go." She runs a hand over the leather bench she's sitting on and then looks back up at me. "He was a horse enthusiast. Loved to ride. I forgot how much fun we used to have here until I sat down, and then all the memories just came flooding back."

I return her smile and nod. "I'm glad then. It's nice when you find a place that brings back happy times."

She nods and sighs softly, her eyes closing for just a moment. "Yes, I suppose it is." When she opens them, her focus is entirely on me. "You're looking quite handsome yourself, Trey. You don't have a date after me, do you?"

I chuff out loud at the thought and shake my head. "No, ma'am! You're my only girl tonight." And I give her a wink, eliciting another laugh from her.

"So, tell me what's new." She lifts a hand to motion to the waiter, who appears immediately and takes our drink order.

"Well, my first day of clinicals is Monday. I'll be jumping in feet to the fire and starting in the emergency room. Should be intense."

"Are you nervous?"

"I guess I should be, but not really. I'm pretty excited actually." The waiter appears and sets a white wine in front of Karen and a whiskey neat in front of me. "I mean, I was a medic over in Afghanistan. I dealt with a lot of trauma. I can't imagine it will be too different."

"Just remember your training and you'll do fine. I know it." She nods confidently and takes a sip of her wine. "And you're sure you still have to work at Temptations? I mean, you're going to be so tired after pulling twelve-hour shifts. You sure you won't reconsider my offer?"

I give her a warm smile, touched by her concern. "I'll work four, twelve-hour shifts but then have three days off in between, so I'll be okay. Once I graduate and make a decent wage, I should be able to quit. It's a means to end. You know that, Karen."

We've discussed this several times, her offering to pay off the balance on my tuition. Which to me was just preposterous. She said she had no children of her own and money to spare and would love to see it put to good use. I turned her down flat. But it's why I love spending time with her. She has no agenda, no ulterior motive. She just truly enjoys my company, and I honestly enjoy hers. My parental figures were less than lacking, and it feels good to have someone to talk to about things in my life, other than Trick of course.

The waiter appears again to take our dinner requests and leaves just as promptly. Karen leans under the table and then places a long rectangular wrapped box in front of me. Before I can even object, her hand is raised to stop me. "It's just a small present to celebrate your clinicals. Don't deny an old woman the pleasure of giving her friend a gift."

I blink in surprise and then nod my head, surrendering to her demand. Honestly, I'm not used to anyone being this nice to me for no reason at all, and I'm speechless. I rest my hand on the box and look up into her sparkling blue ones. "Thank you."

"Well, you have to open it before you can say that," she exclaims with a smile.

I slide the box in front of me and untie the black ribbon before tearing off the gold wrapping paper. I pull the cover off the box and inhale sharply when my eyes land on the wooden box inside before I look back up at Karen, my eyes wide.

"Go on!" She motions for me to continue, a bright smile on her face.

I look back down and trail a finger over the engraved brass plate on the cover of the box:

Trey Riley
Physician Assistant

I pick the exterior box up and turn it over so the wooden box can fall free and then set it flat on the table. I lift the lid on the wooden box and the snap my eyes shut to try and contain the emotion I'm feeling. It's a damn stethoscope. A gorgeous one. I open my eyes and stare at the tool in front of me.

"Do you like it?" she asks, excitement lacing her voice.

I lift my eyes to hers and nod. "Karen, it's—" I stop and clear my throat. "I'm overwhelmed. It's amazing."

Her face beams at my words as she waves toward the box. "Take it out! Let me see how it looks on you."

I graze my fingers over the cool, brass metal, marveling at the camo patterned piping she's managed to find. It's a Littmann, which I know is one of the best on the market, and I'm positive, knowing Karen, it's probably *the* best. I pull it free from its case and hold it up to the light, noticing then that one of the arms is engraved with my name. She's thought of everything.

I fix it around my neck and smile over at her. "How do I look?"

She is literally glowing with pride, making me feel like so much more than the friend I've recently become. Like a mother, proud of her son's accomplishment, something I truly know nothing about but hope it would feel like this. "Like the most handsome doctor in the world."

I reach over and grab her hand in mine. "Thank you, Karen. So much. You have no idea how much this means to me."

She clutches my hand back and squeezes. "The pleasure is all mine, Trey. It really is. I hope you like the camouflage. I thought it would be nice to pay tribute to you as a soldier."

"It's perfect. Really." I place it carefully back in the engraved box and close the lid. "I'm floored."

Just then, the waiter appears with our dinners, so I move the box out of the way, thanking Karen once more. She gives me a final nod and picks up her fork to eat. "So, Trey, think you'll meet any pretty nurses?"

I throw my head back in laughter, the next hour spent eating and talking about everything under the sun.

~Charlotte~

"You ready for the new recruits today? I guess we've got two PAs starting their rounds in our department today." Gabs is leaning over my shoulder, reading the chart of the patient I just did an intake on. "Maybe they'll be hot."

I roll my eyes, even though I know she can't see from her position, but it's a natural reaction to most of the things that come out of her mouth. "Let's just hope they know how to handle traumas. I don't have time to babysit."

"What are their names again?" she asks above me.

I push a couple folders around and find the document posted about the new employees. "Um, Steve Walker and Trey Riley."

"When are they showing up?"

I spin around in the chair and thrust the paper up at her. "Do you read anything that comes across this desk?"

She sticks her tongue out at me and snags the paper from between my fingers. "Yes! Of course, I do! It's just more fun to bug you with twenty questions." She grins mischievously at me and then begins reading the document. "So, it says they'll be here around eight. They're in orientation now with HR. So, the fun begins in about fifteen minutes."

I shake my head and blow out an exasperated breath. "Yes, I'm aware, Gabs. Unlike you, I've read the notice already."

"Whatever, Miss Snooty Pants." She drops the paper back down on the desk and shrugs. "I'm going to check the patients in beds four and eight. Holler if you need me."

"Got it." I return my attention to the chart in front of me, continuing to review it before assigning one of the doctors. I'm pretty sure it's a case of appendicitis and, rather than leave the patient for one of our newbies, I think a more experienced doc may be the right call. I page one of the on-call surgeons I know we'll need and then look out into the waiting room to see who's next.

Intake. My least favorite part of working the E.R. I get to figure out who's drug seeking, who's really sick, and who might be just *kind of* sick. And it's a shit load of paperwork. We rotate the job daily, and today's my lucky day, and on a Monday of all days. Usually one of the busiest. I grab the next form check-in has left for me and call out the name, "Marshall Smith?"

A tall, gangly teenager rises from the waiting area and moves to my window. I buzz him through and reel back from the odor coming from him as he sinks in the chair beside me. Drug user. For certain. I can see track marks all over his arms. "What brings you in today, Marshall?"

He runs a shaky hand over his arms when he sees me looking at them, embarrassment obvious. "I'm not feeling so good."

"Yep, I can see that." I snap a pair of gloves on, then wrap a blood pressure cuff around his arm and flick the switch to take his reading. I lower my voice, wanting him to know I'm here to help and not judge. "When's the last time you used, Marshall?"

His dilated pupils skip up to meet mine, and I can see it hasn't been that long ago. "Maybe a couple hours."

"Okay, so tell me what feels wrong." I pull the cuff off his arm and take his pulse. It's faster than normal, but I'm not surprised by that.

"I feel like I'm about to float out of my body. Everything is dizzy." He shakes his head as if he's trying to clear it. "But it's not like when I'm high. It feels weird."

"Let's get your temperature." I slide the thermometer across his forehead and am surprised when it reads 102.8. "Let me do that one more time, okay?" I take it again and get the same reading. "You use needles, Marshall, or smoke also? Just on your arms? You think you have an infection somewhere?"

"Mostly needles." He looks down at his arms and turns them up then down. "Mostly my arms. Sometimes my feet if I can't find a vein."

I look up at him and give him a sad smile. "Okay, let's get you into a room where we can get a doctor to take a look at you. Can you walk okay?"

He nods his head and stands. "Yeah, I can walk."

I take him through another door and lead him through the examination area until I reach an empty bed. I hand him a gown and then swish the curtain closed, telling him to get changed and then climb into the bed when he's done. He's going to need fluids, and the thought of trying to find a vein on his messy arms makes me blow out a long breath. I turn to grab an I.V. cart and slam right into a hard body.

"Oh!" I stumble back and think I'm about to fall when a strong pair of hands reaches out to hold me steady.

"Whoa! I gotcha!" My head snaps up immediately when I hear the rough voice that belongs to the hands around my arms, my eyes popping wide when I realize who's standing in front of me.

"Maddox?" I shake his hands off me as I absorb that he's actually standing in front of me. In green scrubs. With a cool stethoscope hanging from his neck. Wearing a badge from this hospital. Trey Riley is the name on the badge. What the hell is going on?

"Charlotte?" Disbelief is just as evident in his voice.

CHAPTER NINE

~Trey~

"What are you doing here?" Her brows are furrowed together, a confused expression in her eyes as she tries to piece together my presence here. I see her eyes scan my badge again and I almost groan out loud. *Fuck. Shit's about to get real.*

"I work here." I'm about to say more when a loud clattering and then a thump comes from behind the curtain we're standing in front of.

"My patient!" Alarm sounds in her voice as she rips the curtain back and sprints into action when she sees him on the floor. She slams the code blue call button on the wall, triggering an alert as she races to her patient's side and checks for a pulse. "He's not breathing!"

She points to me and then to a back board on the wall. "Bring that over here."

I grab the board and then fall to my knees on the opposite side of the patient to slide it under him. I look up at her. "Can you lift him?"

She slips her hands into the two slots on her side of the board and nods. "Let's do it on three." She counts down and we both rise in unison, placing the skinny man flat on the bed.

"What's he here for?" I ask, checking again for a pulse and noticing the track marks on his arms.

"Wasn't feeling good. 103 fever. Pressure was a hundred over eighty-nine. Pulse was 120. Said he used a couple hours ago."

"Overdose?" he asks.

She shakes her head. "I don't think so. He walked in here. I think it's something else."

"Well, start compressions. We need blood work. Was it drawn yet?"

She shakes her head again. "No, I was just doing intake. Hadn't gotten that far." I watch as she grabs a stool, stands on it, and then begins compressions. Before I can take another step, the code team arrives and takes over. She gives them the same run-down she just provided to me and then backs away, watching them do their job. I notice Gabby before she notices me, her eyes bugging wide when they finally land on me. *This is going to be a long fucking day.*

"We've got a pulse!" one of the staff shouts and then I hear a slow beeping on the monitor. "Not gonna die today, you little shit." I recognize Gabby's voice on the last statement and can't hide the smile that crosses my face, realizing there's actually a decent human being in there somewhere.

I feel a tug on my arm and turn. Charlotte's little hand tightens around my forearm as she pulls me away from the curtain and down the hall about ten feet. "Are you a doctor here?"

"Physician Assistant," I reply simply. "First day."

Her brow furrows. "We have two new PAs starting today, neither named Maddox." She points to my name tag. "But we do have a Trey Riley."

"Yeah, that would be me." I give her a half-hearted smile and stick my hand out. "Nice to meet you?"

She doesn't take it. She just looks at it and then back up at me.

"Please tell me Maddox is your middle name. Or one of those dumb nicknames you got at a frat house. Or maybe you were in the military?" She points to the stethoscope around my neck, making the connection based on the camouflage design. "A nick name your buddies gave you?"

I run a hand through my hair and shift my stance, spreading my feet wide, the same pose I used to take when I was about to eat shit from one of my drill sergeants. I honestly don't know what the fuck to say to her that's going to make any of this better. And I'm definitely not telling her how I came to meet her in the first place. Of all the fucking luck. She's a goddamn nurse in the hospital I came to work in.

"Just, please, don't tell me you lied to me about your name." Her voice is low now and laced with concern.

"Not exactly." It's the best I can come up with, and I know it's complete shit.

"Not exactly?" She echoes my response, but it's edged with bewilderment.

"Can we talk about this later?" I'm stalling. I know it. She's caught me completely off guard. If it was anyone else, I probably wouldn't even care. But I actually like this girl and care what the hell she thinks. I have to come up with a plausible reason for my dual fucking personality.

"And what the hell should I call you in the meantime?" Her teeth are clenched in frustration as she hisses back at me. "Maddox or Trey? Because I have no idea who the hell you are now!"

I lean in and whisper against her ear, unable to stop myself, even though I know I'm adding fuel to the fire starting to blaze in her. "I'm the guy who made you come twice." She gasps and lifts her walnut eyes to mine. "And now that I know where you are, I hope I can do it again." Her eyes are wide as she looks at me. "Because, Charlotte, I'm still pretty thirsty."

I chuckle as her cheeks flush and then lean in just a little closer, making sure my breath blows across her ear as I speak. "Meet me after work at O'Malley's. I'll explain then." And then I walk away before she can throw any more questions at me.

~Charlotte~

W*hat the hell is going on?* I spin on my heel and stare at his back as he strolls down the hallway and into one of the exam rooms. The cocky bastard didn't even look back. I cross my arms and tap my foot as I wait to see if he comes out in the next minute or two. He doesn't, but Gabby does.

"Gabby!" I call softly, hoping to catch only her attention. I do, because she twists her head and jogs over in my direction.

"Was that who I thought it was?" she squeals out as she approaches.

I bring my fingers to my mouth and bite the edge of one of my nails and nod. "Uh-huh."

"Don't do that! It's gross." Gabby reaches up and yanks my hand out of mouth, sneering. "That was Maddox?"

I nod again. "That was Trey Riley."

Her brows furrow. "Wait, what? Trey Riley our new PA? I thought it was Maddox."

"Yep. He's both, apparently." I snort and plaster a crazy grin on my face. "See! This is why I told you I need to stay away from men." I throw my hands up in the air. "Every. Damn. Time. I give up."

"Maybe Maddox is a nickname or something? Trick's name is really Patrick, so maybe it's like, a thing with them?" She shrugs in thought. "What did he say?"

"He told me to meet him at O'Malley's after our shift." I drum my fingers against my chin and look over at her. "Should I go?"

"Um, yes!" She snaps and then lowers her voice. "You did say it was some of the best sex you ever had!"

73

I look over at her and scrunch my nose up as my thoughts come tumbling out. "I knew he was too good to be true! Too good looking. Too good of a dancer. Too damn good in bed." I snort out loud. "Why couldn't he have just stayed stashed away in a drawer somewhere? A nice, happy memory for me to look back on when I get old?"

"Maybe you can make some new memories with him?" She waggles her brows as she gives me a playful smirk. "Just go see him tonight and see what he has to say."

"Yeah, I'm going to." I shuffle back and forth in place before finally turning and walking back to the front desk to do more intake.

Nine long hours and six Trey-Maddox encounters later, I drag myself into the ladies' locker room to change out of my scrubs. Normally, I'd just go straight to O'Malley's in them, but knowing I'm going to see *whatever his name is* spurs me to try and look a little more human. I change into the sundress I wore when I came in this morning, swipe some mascara over my lashes, and then dab a little gloss on my lips. I pull the elastic out of my hair and then run my fingers through it to try and maintain some order to it. It's loose and shaggy, the layered locks falling around my face. I look in the mirror and force a smile. It's as good as it's going to get after a twelve-hour shift.

I was surprised when Gabby said she'd just meet me at the bar instead of waiting to go over with me, but then she said she might be meeting up with Trick, so I guess I understand. This would be her third time hooking up with him. Unusual for her. I crook my mouth up and wonder if perhaps she may have finally found her match.

I pack my scrubs into my large purse and then slide on a pair of sandals. I leave the locker room and exit the hospital to make the short walk over to O'Malley's. It's just after seven-thirty, but the sun is still out, making it feel earlier. It's the best part of summer around here. The days are finally longer than the nights.

Since it's Monday, I don't expect a crowd when I walk through the door and find I'm correct. I wait a second for my eyes to adjust to the lower lighting and then scan them across the room.

I freeze when my eyes reach the bar, my head tilting as I'm struck with a memory from several weeks ago. Elbows leaning back against the bar, beer in hand, a cocky smile on his face as he stares at me. Holy shit. Maddox is Mr. Sexy Guy. Things just keep getting stranger. Gabby is standing next to him, with who I assume is Trick on the other side of her. *Oh my God.* Mr. Sexy is Trick's friend. I swing my gaze to Gabby, and she knows I've put one and one together.

I blow out a breath and stomp in their direction. Gabby pushes herself off the bar, rushing forward, almost colliding with me as she does. "Did you fucking set this up?" I point a finger to me and then Maddox, or Trey or whatever I'm supposed to call him.

"Don't be mad, Charlie!" She tries to reach a hand out to take my mine, but I take a step back.

"You fucking did!" I seethe out. "I can't believe you fucking did this to me! How could you?"

Not one to ever back down from a fight, Gabby steps right back in my space. "What exactly did I do to you, Charlie? Have a nice guy hit on you? Show you a good time? Tell me! What was so awful about what I did?"

I throw my hands up in the air, not caring that the ten patrons in the bar are all staring at us. "You lied to me! You had me believe it was all random!"

"So what?" she exclaims, turning to point at Trey. "You thought he was hot. He thought you were hot. I thought you'd be hot together." And then she pokes her finger into my chest. "And it was. And you were." She scoffs and takes a step back. "I'm not sorry. It's the happiest I've seen you in months."

My voice quivers as I respond. "But you lied to me, Gabs. You didn't have to do that." I shake my head and, before she can reply, spin on my heel and walk back out of the bar.

75

"Charlie!" I hear her plead after me. "Stop! Please don't go!"

I don't stop though. Not until I'm out the door and two doors down. And I only stop then to pull my sunglasses out of my bag. I slide them over my eyes and blink back the tears threatening to spill over. I push my shoulders back and hold my head up high as I sniffle and spin around to head to the subway, slamming smack into someone for the second time that day.

CHAPTER TEN

~Trey~

"We have to stop meeting like this." I grip her lightly around her forearms to steady her after crashing into me. *Jesus, just touching her again feels good.*

She lets out a small whine as she rests her forehead wearily against my chest and mutters in frustration, "Will this day ever end?"

I slide a finger under her chin and raise it so I can look down at her. "Come on. Let's go get a drink."

She steps back and crosses her arms. "I am not going back in there!"

I slide my hand around her waist and pull her forward as I begin to walk. "I wasn't suggesting that at all. Let's go somewhere we can talk. Okay?"

"Fine." She pouts. I want to bend down and suck her bottom lip into my mouth so badly, but right now is definitely not the time for that. I keep my desire in check and slide my arm around her shoulder instead. I'm surprised when she leans into me and follows my lead.

We only walk a couple blocks when I see a hotel that I know has a lovely bar. I lead us in that direction and then through the sliding doors when we reach it. She stops as we enter the lobby and turns to face me, disbelief painted all over her features. "You brought me to a hotel?"

"They have a nice bar." I nod my head in the direction. "Give me a little credit, Charlotte."

"Oh." One corner of her mouth crooks up as she shrugs. "Sorry."

"Come on." I move my hand to her lower back and guide her through the lobby and into the low-lit bar. I find an empty table in a quiet corner and pull a chair out for her to sit. She does, plopping her bag down on the floor next to her.

I place my hand on her bare shoulder, as soft as I remember, and lean closer to her. "Tequila?"

Her dark eyes turn toward my hand and then trail up the length of my arm until finally latching onto my face. "Just a white wine, please. A Pinot if they have it."

I raise one side of my mouth in a teasing grin. "But you're so much fun when you drink tequila."

She scoffs, but it doesn't hide the faint blush that tints her cheeks. "I'm on again at seven tomorrow."

"Me too." I lift my hand and head toward the bar, commenting as I walk away, "Lucky us." I don't look to see her reaction. I've probably pushed enough of her buttons today, and I do still have to try to get her to understand the whole Maddox name thing.

I order our drinks from the bartender and then carry them back to the table, setting her glass of wine in front of her. I pull out the chair next to her, instead of across from her, and sit. Her brows raise in surprise, I think at my closeness. She's going to have to get over it. If I'm going to be alone with her, I want to be close to her.

"It's Pinot." I point to her glass and then take a sip of the whiskey I ordered for myself.

"Thank you." She takes a large taste, licking her bottom lip as she lowers the glass back to the table. My eyes linger there for a minute before I drag them up to look into her troubled eyes. "So, you knew who I was the whole time?"

Here we go. "Yes." I nod my head.

"Gabby told you to what? Hit on me? Pick me up?" There's a slight edge of doubt to her questions like she still can't believe what she already knows.

"She asked me to come to the event and show you a nice time. That's it." I run my finger around the rim of my glass. "She didn't ask me to sleep with you." I look up at her. "In case you were wondering."

"Why?"

I frown, confused. "Why didn't she ask me to sleep with you?"

She purses her lips then expels a loud breath. "No, genius. Why did she ask you to '*show me a good time*'? Her fingers come up as she makes quotation marks in the air around the last part of her question.

I shrug and look sheepishly away, not wanting to embarrass her. "She said you had a shit ton of bad luck with guys and just wanted to remind you that there were still nice guys around."

"Oh, and you're that nice guy?" She grunts her disagreement. "The one that I now know pretended to like me, proceeded to fuck me, and didn't even tell me his real name?"

My head snaps up at her list of accusations, and I'm about to interrupt, but she slams her hand on the table to stop me. "Do you know how stupid I feel? How used I feel?"

Her voice quivers as she finishes, sending a knife right through my goddamn heart. Hurting her was the last fucking thing I wanted to happen. And the one thing I told Trick from the beginning that I was worried about.

I scoot my chair closer to her in one thump, my thigh lining up against hers, and slide my hand over her cheek to cup it, drawing her face to mine. "Not one thing that happened that night was pretend. *Not one.* Not the way I felt when we danced. Or how my heart sped up when you kissed me. Or how hard you made me when you slipped your dress off. And certainly not the way I felt when I was buried inside of you."

She blinks, her long lashes brushing up against her dusty cheeks as she does. Her mouth opens. Then closes. The opens again. But still she doesn't speak. So, I do what feels natural, and I lean forward and kiss her. She doesn't even resist. Instead, she moans as if giving up and pushes her lips against mine, kissing me back. I pull away after a moment, resting my forehead against hers, and whisper the one thing to her I need to say more than anything. "I'm sorry."

She nods her head against mine as she closes her eyes. When she opens them, it's with another question. "But why did you use the name Maddox? Why not just tell me your real name?"

I straighten then and take a generous sip of my whiskey before I speak. I know this is only going to be a half-truth, and while I'm doing it to lessen the shit storm this has already turned in to, I also know I'm doing it because it's easier than telling her what I really do. Maddox isn't who I am, it's just what I do. "It was just supposed to be me sharing a few dances with you. Maybe a few drinks. Maybe a kiss. Giving a fake name seemed easier. I had no idea when the night started that it was going to end the way it did. No idea it would even matter. And then it was too late. I couldn't tell you after we slept together, and I had no idea that I'd see you again."

"That didn't exactly go as planned, did it?" She spins her wine glass in a small circle and offers me a half smile. *Forgiveness?*

I sigh and drag my fingers through my hair. "Nope. Not exactly." I lower my hand to cover hers, wrapping my fingers around hers, and swing my gaze up to hers. "I am sorry, really sorry that I hurt you. But not about what happened between us."

She sucks her lower lip between her teeth and bites down

gently. She lets go a second later, lowering her gaze as she whispers, "I'm not either."

"Good." I let out a breath that I didn't know I was holding and then lift my hand to hold it in front of her. "I'm Trey. Trey Riley. Can I buy you a drink?"

~Charlotte~

I try, but I can't hide the smile that lifts both corners of my mouth. I want to be mad at him, I really do, but I'm not sure he's the one who's done anything wrong. Gabby is the one who really set this up. And *I* was the one who kissed him first. *I* was the one who took him back to the cottage. Stripped his shirt off. Straddled him. Okay, I feel myself beginning to throb a little and know I need to change the direction of my thoughts.

I slide my hand into the warmth of his and don't pull away when he brings it to his mouth to brush a kiss over my knuckles. "Nice to meet you, Trey." I grace him with a genuine smile as he lowers my hand but doesn't let go. "I'd love another drink, except I have to get up very early tomorrow. Raincheck?"

He cocks his head to the side, a wicked grin lighting up his face, causing his eyes to twinkle. "A raincheck?"

I nod, still smiling, but elaborate for him. "Yes, you know, perhaps another time?"

"How about Friday?"

There isn't a moment's hesitation with his response, and I have to suppress the glee I feel because of it. I nod once instead. "Seven?"

"Just tell me where to pick you up." His voice is a bit darker now.

"Well, you can walk me home if you'd like? Then you'll know. It's not far."

"I'd love to." He releases my hand then and rises from his chair. "Let me just pay the tab."

I watch as he strolls over and gets the bartender's attention. He's wearing faded jeans and, when he leans on the bar, it's hard not to notice how fine his ass looks in them. Holy smokes, that guy is gorgeous. I remember thinking that the night we spent together when he took his shirt off, stunned by his chiseled form, but even with clothes on he's making me hot.

He spins around from the bar and pauses in his tracks when he catches me checking him out. He gives me a cocky grin, his brow arching high, then continues to walk toward me. "I remember that look."

I rise as he approaches and let out a little squeal when he yanks me flush to his body and peers hungrily down at me, practically growling. "If you're going to make me wait until Friday, you better stop. I only have so much restraint."

I think he's going to kiss me. I blink up at him and hope he's going to kiss me. He lets out a slow breath and chuckles instead. "What I'd like to do to you right now." His fingers tighten on my waist as he narrows his eyes. "You're killing me in this little dress." And then he releases me, planting a soft kiss on my forehead as he does. He steps back, bringing a hand to the back of his neck with a grimace and nods at the floor. "Don't forget your bag."

I stare at him blankly for a moment then lower my gaze to the floor, my over-sized purse at my feet. I bend to pick it up. "Where was my head?" I murmur, still in a bit of a daze from the moment we just shared.

He threads his hand in my free one and heads in the direction of the exit. "Come on."

It's gotten dark and it takes me a minute to get my bearings and figure out where we are so I know which direction to go in, but then turn to the left. "I live off 18th, close to 9th Ave."

He pulls me to a stop. "That's like twenty blocks from here. You walk that every day?"

"Subway," I respond like it should be obvious.

"I'll call an Uber." He grabs his phone from his pocket and is sliding his fingers over the screen before I can even object. "Not that I don't want to spend twenty blocks of time with you." He smiles sexily. "But I'm tired. And I live in Tribeca. So, I'm gonna need one anyway."

"You live in Tribeca?" My brows shoot up in surprise. It's a pricey neighborhood. He didn't strike me as coming from money.

He laughs out loud, knowing exactly what must be running through my mind. "Don't worry. I'm not some secret prince." He slides his phone back in his pocket. "Trick's grandmother owns the building. I share a place with him and she's good to us."

"Is Trick a PA, too? Because if he shows up at the hospital tomorrow, shit's really going to hit the fan," I joke, trying to bring some humor to what occurred earlier in the day.

He chuckles and scratches his chin. "Yeah, no worries there. I'm lucky if I can get his ass off the couch lately." He gives me a look that hints at something deeper and then continues. "We served together over in Afghanistan. I was a medic. He was a chopper pilot." He shrugs. "Shit happened. He's still processing."

"I'm sorry." I step closer and link my fingers back through his, tilting my head to look up at him. "Are you okay? Did you get hurt over there?" I don't remember seeing any scars on his body, but I also knew the internal injuries are generally far worse and more lingering.

His fingers weave up into my hair as he leans down, his lips turned up in a small smile, before he presses them lightly to mine. I want to turn it into so much more, but he draws away after just a second. "I'm fine." He places another soft kiss against my mouth then stands up straight. "Thanks."

A car pulls up to the curb next to us and, seeing the Uber sticker in the back window, we know it's our ride. He opens the door and we both slide into the back seat. Once the door is shut, the driver zooms back out into traffic. "You want to be closer to 10th or 9th?"

"9th please," I respond and then look down when I feel heat land just above my bare knee then fingers brushing gently against the inside of my leg. I turn my eyes up and still when I'm met by dark, lust filled irises staring back at me. I lick my lips in preparation for what I want to come next.

He smirks, knowing exactly what I need, but doesn't comply. He bends his head so his lips brush against my ear instead. "Friday feels like a very long time away."

His hand fans out as he moves it just a fraction higher, my legs reacting on their own, spreading wider, heat searing straight to my core. He chuckles, the vibration against my ear sending tingles over my body. "Especially if you keep biting your lip like that."

I twist my head so that my lips almost touch his, my breath hot as it leaves my mouth, and lock my gaze with his. I run my tongue teasingly over my lower lip then drag it slowly back through my teeth, watching his pupils dilate as I do. I place my hand over his and, instead of pushing it away, force it to slide further up my thigh. He sucks in a small hiss of surprise, and unable to stop, I lean forward and dart my tongue out, swiping it against his upper lip.

"Yes, Friday is definitely a long time away." I scoot my hips forward, causing his hand to slide higher, and fight back a moan when I feel a finger brush up against the silk of my panties.

His forehead falls against mine, and he lets out a hot breath. "Sweet Jesus, Charlotte." Then he surges the short distance to my mouth, crashing his lips against mine, his entire hand sliding at the same time to cup my pussy. His other hand latches onto the back of my neck and hauls my chest to his, my arms lifting to wrap around his shoulders.

I pray that the driver thinks we're just kissing, but even if he suspects we're doing more, it doesn't stop me from thrusting my core against the ball of Trey's hand. I whimper against his lips when he shifts his hand and presses two fingers against my clit and rubs. I want to climb on top of him and grind against his cock but fist his t-shirt instead, trying to tamp down the animalistic need he brings out in me.

Just when I think I'm about to combust, Trey tightens the grip on my neck and pulls his lips off mine, his fingers leaving my core to slide back down my leg. I let out a small gasp of protest, which is promptly responded to with a small chuckle as he lays his cheek against mine.

"If I'm going to make you come, Charlotte, it's going to be some place I can hear you scream." I suck in a sharp breath, my pussy convulsing just at the thought he evokes, and nod my head, unable to respond verbally.

"Besides, we're here." He draws back from me and points out the window then shifts his attention to the driver. "Just give me a minute to walk her to her door. I'll be two minutes."

"Yep. No problem," the driver replies.

I manage to exit the vehicle on legs that feel like jelly and walk past three buildings, stopping at the stairwell leading to my mine. His hand, which has been on my lower back, slides upward until it latches loosely onto the back of my neck. He tips my head back and drops his mouth to mine in a searing kiss. The two-hundred foot walk to my building was not nearly long enough to dampen the desire building between us. I grab the front of his shirt and fist it as I pull myself closer to him, wanting to feel him against me again. I'm just shy of wrapping my leg around him and humping him like a dog when he tears his mouth from mine and pushes me back gently, a small groan escaping him as he does.

"I think my two minutes are up." He gives me an apologetic grin and then turns, waving once as he does. "See you in the morning, Charlotte."

I'm not even sorry when I stare shamelessly at his ass as he strolls away.

CHAPTER ELEVEN

~Trey~

My cock is still throbbing like a mother fucker when I enter my apartment and call out to see if Trick's home. I'm relieved when he doesn't answer because I'm not in the mood to deal with him or his bullshit right now. All I want is to take a hot shower to try to alleviate some of the sexual tension between my legs.

I stride into my bedroom, stripping my shirt off as I go, and then pop the button on my jeans. I throw the shirt in a clothes basket in the corner and then push my jeans down and off my legs, throwing them in next. I grab a clean towel off a shelf in my closet and walk naked back through the living room to the bathroom, my dick bobbing against my stomach the whole time.

I slam the door shut behind me, turn the tap on hot, and then step under the streaming water. It takes it a minute to start warming up but less than that for my hand to find its way around my cock. *Sweet Jesus what this girl does to me.* I don't think anyone has ever given me a hard-on that's lasted thirty-two goddamn blocks.

I let the water run down my body while moving my hand up and down my length, the hot moisture reminding me of her mouth. I close my eyes, letting my head fall back as I remember exactly what it felt like when she sucked my cock into her mouth and swallowed. My dick jerks in my hand at the memory, and I squeeze it hard, groaning from the pressure.

I loosen my grip and stroke up to my crown then tighten my fist. This is what it felt like when her pussy clenched around me as I slid inside of her. I drag my fist down my cock and then slide it back up again, a low growl sounding from my chest as I feel my release start to build. I work my hand faster up and down my length, one hand slamming against the wall of the shower as I roar out my release, her name tumbling from my lips as I pant in relief.

I stay like that for several long minutes, waiting for my heartrate to slow down. I finally open my eyes and push myself off the wall, my thoughts no clearer than they were twenty minutes ago. She's invaded every corner of my mind since she slammed into me this morning. It had been over ten days since I'd seen her, but one touch made it feel like it was yesterday. From her soft, citrusy smell that assaulted my nostrils when her hair flew up under my chin, to how little her frame was when I reached to keep her from falling.

She was a little slice of heaven I had relived more than once since I was with her, but one I didn't think I'd get to experience again. Seeing her today changed everything. And what makes it all worse is that she still doesn't know the complete truth about me. Frankly, I'm surprised she gave in so easily and forgave me for my part in the deceit we played in 'showing her a good time' for a night. If she's someone I want to keep seeing, and right now things sure seemed to be headed in that direction, sooner or later, she's going to know the whole truth about me.

Right now, there is no way I can walk away from Temptations. I still owe way too much on my loans, and even though Trick and I rent from his grandmother, it still isn't cheap. I shake the water from my hair as I step from the shower and grab my towel, sluicing off my wet skin before wrapping it around my waist. I take a piss, brush my teeth, and then exit the bathroom.

I'm surprised when I see Trick sitting on the sofa, a soda in his hand for once instead of a beer. He's sitting in just his jeans, sans shirt, staring blankly at the television screen, the volume muted. "Didn't expect you to be home so early."

"Wanted to make sure you were okay." His voice is low and monotone.

I move past him into my bedroom and talk on the way. "I'm fine. Why wouldn't I be?"

"You left with that girl. Charlene or whatever."

I pull on a pair of sleep pants and go back into the room so I can talk to him, face-to-face. "Charlotte. You know her name is Charlotte."

"Whatever," he retorts.

"Why the fuck do you even care? Gabby throw you to the curb?" I'm being a dick, but I'm still pissed off that I somehow got caught in the middle of all of this, and it was all so he could get laid again by the crazy bitch.

"You know I could have fucked her again whether you did this for me or not, right?" He looks up at me, his jaw clenched. "I saw it the minute you laid eyes on her in that bar the first time. I did you the favor here."

"Oh, really?" I scoff. "What kind of favor do you think you did for me exactly?"

He rises off the couch and turns to face me. "When's the last time you let anybody in your life? Dated someone that you weren't paid to date?"

"What the fuck is that supposed to mean?" I cock my head in confusion.

"I could tell you liked her. Gabby said she definitely liked the looks of you. We both thought…" He lifts his shoulders and shrugs past me. "I don't know, that maybe you'd be good for each other."

I spin around and am about to dig into him some more but pause when I see the tattoo across his shoulders. *All Pain Is Fleeting.* I close my eyes for a second, realizing that this was his way, Trick's way, of trying to do something nice for me. As fucked up as it all is. That just isn't something he does very often.

I blow out a breath, reining my temper back a notch, and walk forward to slap him on the shoulder. "Next time, just be straight up with me. I can get my own dates, brother."

He nods his head once and then keeps walking until he crosses the threshold to his bedroom and shuts the door quietly behind him. I've had about all the damn drama I can stand for one night, so I shut all the lights off in our apartment and follow suit, heading to my own bedroom. I shut the door and then crawl under the covers, thinking again of Charlotte before sleep takes me away.

~Charlotte~

"I don't care if you buy me ten lattes and have them served to me by the King of Persia. I'm still pissed at you, Gabby!" I close and lock the door to my apartment and then stomp down the stairs to the sidewalk.

She runs after me, trying to keep up as I maintain a brisk pace to the subway station. It's a half-hour before our shift and I don't want to be late. I'm not going to stand here on the sidewalk and argue with her again about what she did to me. She kept me up half the night with endless texts begging for forgiveness and then showed up at my doorstep this morning bearing designer cup lattes. *I ain't that fucking easy.*

"Charlie, I said I'm sorry. A hundred times! I honestly thought

I was doing something nice for you!" She continues to plead her case as she scurries along next to me.

I halt in my tracks and glare over at her. "By deceiving me! By tricking me into sleeping with someone!" I begin moving forward again.

"No! I honestly just wanted you to have a nice time with a guy I knew you thought was hot." She lets out a small chortle of laughter. "I mean, I hoped you'd get laid, too, but it wasn't part of the deal."

I shake my head and throw my hands up in the air. "You just don't get it! I mean, seriously, Gabby!"

"But you liked him. And you had fun," she whines in defense. "I don't see what the big frigging deal is!"

"Because you LIED to me, Gabrielle!" I turn my head and practically snarl at her. "My best friend should not lie to me."

She grabs me by the arm and pulls me to a stop, her features growing serious. "Charlie, I'm sorry. Really sorry. I fucked up. I thought I was doing something good for you. I never meant for it to be something dirty." She looks down then, blinking rapidly, scuffing her sneakered foot against the pavement.

"Argh!" I yell. "Why do I have to love you so much!" I grab her hand in mine and yank it as I begin walking again. "You better promise to never, ever, ever pull something like this again, because—"

"I swear!" She squeezes my hand with both of hers and holds it over her heart. "I swear, Charlie. On my life. Never again."

"And it wasn't dirty," I proclaim, referring to her earlier comment.

She squeezes my hand. "I know, doll. I know."

We're quiet until we get on the subway, and then she finally bursts with questions I know she's been dying to ask. "So, what happened after you left last night? Did you talk to him? Are you going to see him again?"

I give her a sheepish smile and then tell her everything, right down to our very naughty Uber ride. We giggle the rest of the ride and walk into work with huge smiles on our faces. We head directly to the locker room and change quickly. We've only got five minutes to spare and need to go over all the patient charts with the outgoing staff for shift change.

I'm thrilled that I'm not working intake today, especially after yesterday. Mondays are always busy with the people who don't want to come in over the weekend, so Tuesdays usually offer a little relief. Not that I'm sure it really matters. Every day is busy around here. I grab two of the charts for patients already in beds and head in their direction to check on them.

"Oh, nurse, do you have a minute?"

I grin at the husky voice behind me and then wipe it off before I turn around. "Can I help you?"

"Yes, the door is locked and I need to get in there." He takes a step closer to me, pointing to the closet where the linens are kept.

"Making beds now? I don't think that's something we normally ask of our PA's, but it's nice of you to chip in."

"Actually, I need some fresh scrubs." He points to the bottom of his shirt that I can now see is covered in something yellow and slimy.

"Yuck." I grimace. "Yes, in that case, let's see if I can help you." I glide past him and then look over my shoulder, crooking my finger as I go, not missing the playful gleam in his eyes.

I use my access card to swipe the lock on the door and then pull it open. I enter, feeling him close on my heels, snapping the light switch on as I go. The door slams shut and I wheel around, almost banging into him.

"Morning." His voice is husky and I watch mesmerized as he reaches a hand behind his head to grip his shirt and then pull it off.

Why does he have to be so goddamn delicious looking when he does that? I try to keep my eyes focused on his but fail miserably and drag them down his torso instead. I do maintain some composure and manage to keep my hands from reaching out to run over his bumpy abdomen. "Morning," I squeak out then clear my throat.

He slides a finger under my chin and lifts my gaze up to meet his. "I couldn't stop thinking about you last night."

I just nod, my voice seemingly lost as my heart begins to thunder in my chest, understanding exactly how he felt.

He chuckles. "Cat got your tongue?" He moves his thumb up to skim across my bottom lip and leans closer, whispering in that sexy voice of his, "I can probably help with that." And then, so softly, he skims his lips against mine, not once, not twice, but three times, until I rise up on the tips of my toes and thrust my mouth against his.

His hand grabs onto the ponytail I'm wearing and yanks my head back as he begins nipping gently down my neck until he reaches the V in my scrubs. He kisses the heart of my cleavage and then licks a long trail back to my mouth, fusing his to mine again. I moan his name as my fingers clutch onto the bare skin of his shoulders and then yelp in complaint when he suddenly releases me.

He's panting lightly as he stares down at me, a dark gleam in his eyes that whispers of something darker. Something that I haven't seen yet. His grip on my hair relaxes, and his fingers drag across my head, down to my cheek, and then gently cup my cheek for a second before letting go. He lifts his brows as he stares at me, puffing out a deep breath as he shakes his head. "Sweet Jesus."

He reaches on the top shelf behind me to pull down a shirt and chuckles. "Still feels like I'm in the damn desert." Then he pivots around, pushing out the door, shoving the shirt over his head as he goes. "So fucking thirsty," is all I hear before the door clicks closed.

CHAPTER TWELVE

~Trey~

It's been the longest week ever. But also one of the best I've had in a long time. I love being in the E.R., in the action again. Seeing patients, dealing with the traumas, and even the cases that don't require much effort makes me feel like I'm serving a purpose again. And, of course, there's Charlotte. I don't know how many stolen kisses we've shared this week; all I know is that each next one was hotter than the one before.

And it's finally Friday. I can't wait to be alone with her, outside of the hospital, and hopefully get to know her a little better. And I don't just mean carnally, although I sure as hell am hoping for that also. I know nothing about where she's from, her family, or what she does when she's not at the hospital. Every stolen moment I spend with her is amazing, but I want more than that. At least, I'm pretty sure I do.

I'm in the back of Gene's car and nervous about whether or not I should have used him to pick us up. Will she question why I have a private car, as opposed to the Uber or taxi most people in our financial position would have done? And will that lead to me having to explain what else I do for a living? I'm not ready to go there yet. At least, not until I figure out where and if *we* are actually even going anywhere.

I wasn't sure what to do for our date. I wanted it to be special. Something that was of our own doing as opposed to the set-up our friends had already arranged. So, I called Karen and asked her for advice. I wanted old school. I wanted romantic. I wanted to sweep her off her damn feet. She was delighted to help me, of course, but only after she made me promise to tell her everything about Charlotte. Then she also demanded a report of this date next week when we have our regular dinner. It wasn't really a hard bargain, so I took it willingly. She helped get me reservations at The Rainbow Room and told me the best places to take her dancing.

Gene pulls up in front of her building and puts the car in park, moving to open his door.

"It's okay, Gene." I push my door open, taking the bouquet of pink flowers I brought her as I leave. "Stay in the car. I'll be out shortly."

"Yes, sir."

I'm not even going to try to correct him. It would do no good. I stride across the sidewalk and then gingerly up the stairs to the landing and press the buzzer to apartment four as she instructed.

I hear a short buzz and then her hollow voice in the speaker. "Is it you?" She sounds out of breath.

I press the talk button. "It's me. If that's the you, you mean."

I hear static and then a short giggle. "It's me. Come up."

The lock on the door clicks and disengages, so I pull it open and walk up the stairs. It looks like there are two apartments on each floor, so I'm assuming I only need to go up one flight. When I reach the top of the second flight, I look to the right and confirm my thoughts when I see the number four on one of the doors.

I approach the door and rap twice, surprised at the nerves bouncing around in my stomach. I can hear footsteps clicking on the other side then locks being turned before the door eventually swings open. I let out a low whistle of appreciation when I see her, bowled over by her beauty again. "Wow."

Her cheeks immediately flush pink as she shuffles in place before realizing I'm still standing in the hallway "Oh, come in! Sorry!"

She takes a step back so I can move inside. As I do, I take the flowers I'm holding and extend them to her. "For you."

Her face lights up at the simple gesture as she slips them from my hands, clutching them to her chest as she buries her nose in the blooms and inhales deeply. She looks back up at me beaming. "Did Gabby tell you?"

"Tell me what?" I step in and shut the door behind me, honestly not sure what she means.

"Peonies are my favorite." She smells them again, the happiness in her face only growing.

"No." I take a step closer to her and brush my fingers lightly over the soft petals of the flowers. "When I saw them, they reminded me of the dress you had on that first night we met. At least, the skirt of the dress."

"Ohhh." She's looks at me dreamily and then snaps out of it, turning her attention back to the flowers. "Well, thank you. They are absolutely beautiful."

"Speaking of beautiful." I take two steps to close the distance between us, tug the flowers from her hands, and step back from her. "Turn around for me."

Her head tilts to the right as she anchors a foot in place and twirls in a slow circle. The skirt of the burgundy dress she's wearing reaches only to mid-thigh in the front but is longer in the back and flares up as she moves. The top is fitted and runs straight across her chest, her shoulders bare, with just a tiny bit of cleavage exposed. She wears a simple silver chain around her neck with matching hoop earrings. The black strappy heels she's wearing are tied tightly with silk around her ankles and might be some of the sexiest shoes I've ever seen. As she completes her rotation, she lifts her hands out to her sides, palms up, stopping as she shrugs her shoulders.

"No." I set the flowers on a table beside me and stride to close the distance between us, bringing my hands up to cradle her face. "Don't do that. Don't doubt how unbelievable you look." I lock my eyes with hers so she can see how serious I am. I brush a kiss against her darkened lips, tasting fresh mint on her breath. "You're exquisite."

"Thank you," she replies softly, placing one tiny hand on the arm of my jacket, trailing it slowly up its length as her gaze sweeps over my frame before locking onto my face. "You're looking mighty fine yourself." Her hand tightens around my bicep. "Although, I've become rather partial to seeing these in your scrubs every day. They're a bit hidden in here."

I grin wickedly. "Don't worry, I'm sure we can fix that." I lean down and place a longing kiss against her lips. "Later." The edges of my smile curl higher when I see the disappointment in her eyes. "We have reservations and our ride is waiting."

"Our ride?" Her brows rise.

"I've arranged a car for the evening. Much easier than Uber." Before she can question me further, I release my hold on her and reach for the flowers. "Why don't you put these in water before we go though, so they don't die?"

"Good idea." She takes them from me and turns to go to the kitchen I can see from here. I watch as she walks away, her heels making soft clicking sounds as she retreats, her skirt swishing against her legs. Just thinking about how I want to lift that skirt as she bends into the cabinet to reach for a vase has my cock hardening. I blow out a yearning breath and focus my attention on the rest of her apartment instead.

It's not large by any means. I'm standing in the main living area, which is a large square, and can see only three other doorways. One, which is open, clearly leads to the bathroom. The other two are closed. I'm assuming bedrooms? Maybe one is a closet? I hope to find out later which one leads to her room. Before I can investigate further, she's standing back in front of me with a black silk clutch in hand. "Ready?"

I nod and place my hand on her lower back, my fingers grazing the silk of her skin. "Let's go."

~Charlotte~

Only because he warned me, I'm not completely surprised when we exit my building and there's a gentleman waiting next to a black town car. As we descend the stairs, he pulls the back door open, greeting us both warmly. "Good evening."

I offer him a polite smile as I climb into the car and slide across the smooth leather seat to make room for Trey. I've had drivers before; it's pretty much a requirement if I go anywhere with Gabrielle. Though she tries really hard not to be the princess she is, she detests public transportation. But, never have I had a private driver on a date. Trey said he didn't come from money, but this makes me wonder. I don't want to overthink it, though, and instead concentrate on the way his fingers are grazing softly over my palm resting in his hand.

"Do I get to know where we're going yet?" I swipe my free hand down one side of my skirt then nudge him with my shoulder. "You didn't make it very easy for me to figure out what I should wear."

His dark eyes rake over my body. "I promise, you're perfect." His tongue darts out to moisten his dry lips that turn up at one corner when he notices me watching. "Why is it so hard to stop doing this?" And then he fuses his lips to mine, a small moan escaping from me when his fingers dig into my thigh. He uses this to his advantage and sweeps his tongue inside to tangle with mine.

I grasp onto the lapel of his jacket and drag him closer,

wanting more of him. Always wanting more. This week has been filled with endless, mindless kissing and it's not enough. He chuckles at my urgency but complies, wrapping a hand around my waist to pull me flush, severing his lips from mine to move them to my ear. "I know, baby. I know..." comes out in a hot breath, my head falling back as he latches his mouth onto my neck and sucks gently, lifting and moving lower and lower until he's at the top of my shoulder.

I can feel my nipples tightening against the fabric of my dress as my core starts to throb, and I slide my hand over his lap until it finds his length, bulging against the soft material of his pants. I'm so relieved to know that I make him as wanton as he makes me. I wrap my hand around him and squeeze softly, wanting so badly for my mouth to be what surrounds him right now instead.

He lets out a growl so low only I can hear, but the emotion behind it screams desire. His hand falls over mine and contracts around it tightly, his cock jerking hard, air hissing through his teeth, before he wrenches my hand off him. His mouth crashes against mine in a devouring kiss as he forces both of my hands in my lap and holds them there. When he breaks away from me, he's panting, his eyes consumed with lust as they latch onto mine. "I'm going to fuck you right here in this car if we don't stop."

My pussy literally contracts. I can feel moisture pooling between my legs so I press them together to try and quench some of the longing, when I really want to beg him not to stop. "You kissed me," I defend, pulling my bottom lip between my teeth, biting down.

His eyes dart to my mouth, eliciting another growl. "And stop doing that." He swipes a kiss across my mouth, forcing me to release my lip. "I'm taking you to a nice dinner before I fuck you. Got it?"

"Uh-huh," I tumble out, nodding my head, pressing my legs even tighter, hoping the thin scrap of material I'm wearing won't drip from how wet he's making me.

"Good." He puffs out a breath, relaxing his grip on my hands, and then adjusts himself so he's leaning back against the seat again. "Sweet Jesus, you're dangerous," he mutters, closing his eyes as he tries to catch his breath.

"You kissed me," I squeak out once more in defense

His eyes open as he twists his head to look at me, sultry and full of sin. "And I'm going to do it again. I promise. But, next time, I'm not stopping."

Holy shit. This is not helping the panty situation one bit. I stare back at him, swallowing back the arousal he's woken in me, and nod my head. "As long as you promise."

His eyes flare and he snorts in laughter. "You may just be the one that ruins me for everyone else, Charlotte."

"Sir?" A deep voice echoes from the front of the vehicle. "We're here."

I look out my window and see we're on 5th Ave., at Rockefeller Center to be exact, and turn quizzically back to Trey. "This is very uptown."

"I wanted to do something special." He winks at me and then steps out of the door the driver is holding open, extending his hand to assist me as I slide out. He tells the driver we'll be an hour or two and he'll text when we're ready for the car, and then comes to stand next to me on the sidewalk.

He points at the Rockefeller building. "Have you been up there? To the Rainbow Room?"

He places his hand on my back and guides me down the wide walkway, past the small fountains trickling quietly in the center, toward the very tall building. "Never." I turn and look at him. "Isn't it impossible to get in here unless you know someone?"

"Guess I know someone then." He chuckles softly. "We're going up to Bar SixtyFive. The views are supposed to be spectacular."

I'm a bit overwhelmed with just how spectacular this night has gone so far, and it really hasn't even started yet. I know I was pissed at Gabby for her whole set-up game, but I'm thinking now that I need to kiss the ground she walks on the next time I see her. We enter the building and he leads me to an elevator on the other side of the lobby, manned by a very official looking individual.

"Good evening, sir, miss." He nods his head at both of us. "Are you dining at one of the establishments?"

"We have a reservation under Riley, for seven-thirty, at Bar SixtyFive."

I know it's silly, but hearing how confident and in control Trey is and has been so far this evening sends a shiver of excitement right down my spine. It's sexy as hell and a feature that's been lacking in so many other men I've dated. I feel like, maybe for the first time, I'm actually with a man, and one who knows how to take care of me.

The attendant checks the computer in front of him, punches something in on the keyboard, then directs his attention back to us. "Right this way."

I slip my hand into the crook of Trey's arm and follow the attendant as he pushes a button for the elevator and then sweeps his arm wide when the doors open, indicating we should enter. "Just hit number sixty-five. Have a nice evening."

The door slides shut as Trey punches the button and steps back to stand beside me. He glides his hand lightly across my bare back and then stops, resting his hand on the back of my neck, just below my hairline. I shift slightly so I can look up at him and find him already peering down at me.

"I'm not going to do it." He continues to stare at me.

"Do what?" I ask innocently, knowing full well what he means.

His mouth cocks up on one side, his head moving slowly back and forth as a low chuckle escapes. "I'm not going to kiss you." He leans into me then and brushes his nose against my cheek until his lips are a breath away from my ear. "Not until I don't have to stop."

I giggle and am about to respond, but the elevator jolts to a quick stop, pausing my thought as the doors slide open. Instead, I gasp softly at the opulent room in front of me. The entire room is lined in long, plate glass windows that showcase the glorious New York City skyline and beyond. "Oh my gosh, it's beautiful!" I whisper to Trey.

"It really is," he agrees and directs me forward to another podium that has a pretty hostess waiting for us. "Mr. Riley?"

He nods his head in acknowledgement.

She slides two menus off a shelf behind her and then sashays out from the podium and begins walking into the restaurant. "Right this way. Your table is ready."

I almost gasp again when she leads us to a spectacular table up against one of the windows, boasting a view words can't describe, but somehow, I manage to maintain my dignity and simply lower myself in the chair that Trey is holding out for me. She places a menu in front of me then does the same for Trey once he's seated. "Amy will be your server this evening and will be with you in just a moment. Have a lovely dinner."

"Thank you," Trey and I both say in unison as she glides back to her station.

"Wow." I have to say it at least once before the waitress comes. I look out the window to absorb the view before turning back to Trey, my mouth open in wonder.

"I'm trying to be cool here, but," he lowers his voice, "this is fucking amazing, right?" He's as blown away as I am and I love it. I love his honesty and that he's not afraid to share in this experience with me instead of trying to play it off like it's just another average night for him.

I bob my head up and down. "Amazing." My cheeks hurt I'm smiling so hard, but I just can't help it. "Thank you for this."

"I have to thank my friend Karen," he replies, also smiling.

"Karen?" I try to keep my smile relaxed as a stab of jealousy slices through me.

"She's a friend I met through work. She's amazing. A widow

who lost her husband a year ago. They spent their hey-days growing up with the city, and she knows so much about so many places." His eyes are twinkling as he describes her, his admiration for her evident. He taps a finger on the table. "She was the one who got us a reservation here. So, I'll thank her for both of us."

"Please do." I smile genuinely now. "She sounds lovely. And interesting!"

"You should hear the stories she tells." He shakes his head. "To have lived here through the fifties, sixties, and seventies. I can't even imagine."

Before I can reply, a smartly dressed woman stops beside our table. "Can I wish you both a good evening? I'm Amy and will be your server."

We spend the next half hour ordering drinks, then an appetizer, and finally our meals. We both share tidbits about the week at work, about Gabby and Trick, and then finally more personal details when our meal is served.

He cuts a piece of his steak and looks over at me. "Tell me about you. Where did you grow up? Tell me about your family."

Talking about my parents has become one of my least favorite subjects, but I know it's a bridge that needs to eventually be crossed in every relationship when you're in the 'getting to know you' phase. I push the fish I've ordered around on my plate and let out a small sigh before looking up at him. "I'm not one of those girls who has a happy childhood to lament over. So, I'm just going to make this quick, okay?"

His brows furrow but he nods his head. "Okay."

"The first ten years of my life weren't so bad actually. I have really good memories from that time. Lived in a little house in Philly with my younger sister. My mom and dad were really happy. But then my mom died. She was killed when another car hit hers in a snow storm." I shift in my seat and take a sip of my wine. 'Til this day, her being ripped from my life so abruptly still hurts.

"My dad wasn't the same after that. He started drinking a lot, and we eventually lost the house and had to move to the projects. He tried really hard to be a good dad, but he just couldn't get past my mom's death. My sister ran wild, and I just tried to keep all the pieces together." I look up at him with sad eyes. "I spent most of my teenage years taking care of my dad, and trying to get through school. I moved here after nursing school. A few months after that, I found out my dad was sick. He died. Just a few months ago. Liver cancer. My sister didn't even show up to the funeral, so I just kinda feel like I'm on my own." I talk fast and, when I'm done, pick up my glass of wine and take a large sip, afraid to see what his reaction may be.

When I look up, he's staring at me, a serious look on his face. He lifts his hand and runs it down his face as he shakes his head once. "I'm sorry. None of that sounds like it was easy."

This time, it's him who lifts his drink, and instead of taking a sip, he drains what's left of the whiskey. He sets the glass softly on the table and nods at me. "Small world though. I grew up in Philly, too. Over in Hunting Park. And while we lived in a house, I'm not really sure it should have been called that. A shack maybe. I used to think it was going to cave in on us during the winter when the wind was howling."

"Yeah, it wasn't much better where we lived in Fairhill. The wind felt like it went right through our apartment, and ninety percent of the time, it was already freezing because the heat didn't work. Those were some fun times." I recall sarcastically.

"My dad would beat the shit out of me at least twice a month. I don't even know what for. He would just come home drunk and pissed and take it out on me. When I got old enough, I started hitting him back. When I was fifteen, I hit him so hard he was unconscious for six hours. I honestly didn't know if he was going to wake up. I thought I might have killed him."

He raises his glass, signaling Amy for a refill, and looks back at me. "My mom was just as bad, but at least she didn't hit me." He shrugs. "So, when I was seventeen, I signed up for the Army, and two weeks after I graduated high school, I was on a bus to basics."

"I'm sorry." I'm not sure what for, but I feel like it needs to be said.

Amy stops at our table and sets a fresh tumbler of whiskey in front of Trey, swapping it for the empty. "You two okay? Need anything else?"

We both shake our heads and smile. "Thank you, no."

"So, had enough family history?" I joke, taking a sip of my wine, smiling around the rim of my glass.

"Uh, yeah," he chides back. "That got depressing fast, didn't it?"

"A little. But, hey, no worries about whose house we're having Thanksgiving dinner at!"

"Cheers to that." He laughs out loud and lifts his glass to clink it against mine. "I'll probably be working anyway. You know us first year PAs are going to get stuck with all the holidays."

"I'll bring you a piece of pumpkin pie if you are." I give him a playful wink as relief washes over me that the mood is steering back to something lighter again. We spend the rest of dinner and then dessert talking about the respective schools we went to, how old we are, when our birthdays are, and analyzing all our favorites. All the things we probably should have covered before we slept together, but of course, given the circumstances, didn't.

Amy brings our bill, which Trey pays, and we make our way out of the restaurant, take the elevator down, and head back outside. It's beautiful out, the temperature still warm, even though the sun is now gone over the horizon.

Trey slides his arm around my waist and pulls me up against him, slipping a finger under my chin to tilt it up to his face. "I was going to take you dancing, but I really just want to be some place alone with you. Some place I don't have to share you with anyone else."

My lips curve up and I nod slowly. "I have an idea."

"Let's go." He releases me and pulls his phone out of his pocket. "Let me call Gene."

"Gene?"

"My driver." He begins pressing buttons on his phone, but I hold my hand over the screen to stop him for a second.

"Dismiss him." I lift my hand off the screen. "We can walk."

CHAPTER THIRTEEN

~Trey~

I look down at her feet, criss-crossed with satin, on heels that are at least three inches tall, and raise my brows. "You sure?"

She grabs my hand and starts walking toward Fifth. "I'm positive. It's close."

I take one long stride so I'm walking beside her and grasp her hand more firmly. I don't mind if she leads, but I still like to be beside her. She heads left once we reach the street and leans against me as we walk.

"You're sure you're okay in those?" I ask again, looking dubiously at the pointy heels.

"I'm fine!" She laughs and then motions down the street. "I can walk a few blocks in these; it's not going to kill me. Besides, it's right down there."

The only thing I can think of in that direction is the park, and I'm not sure how safe it is after dark. We cross over a larger intersection and make our across the front of The Plaza, passing the large fountain that stands in front as we walk.

"Have you figured it out yet?" she teases.

"No, I don't think so."

"Gah!" She laughs out loud. "What's one of the most romantic things to do in New York City in the summer?"

We've reached the edge of the park now, and as I look ahead, it finally dawns on me as I see the carriages lined up, horses neighing impatiently. I look over at her and smile broadly. "I love it."

"Really?" She beams back at me. "It's a good night for it. Can I tell you a secret?" She leans closer to me and whispers. "I've lived here for four years and I've never taken a ride in one!"

"Well, tonight's the night then." I pull her toward the line of carriages and look over at her. "Any one in particular that catches your fancy?"

She peruses the line-up and then pauses, pointing her finger toward a shiny, white carriage. "That one." She nods her head and giggles. "I may as well satisfy my Cinderella dreams at the same time."

"Well, I'm not sure if I'm quite up to Prince Charming status, but I'll see what I can do." I wink at her and then approach the driver to arrange our ride. Five minutes later, we're both sitting comfortably in the carriage, and our driver, Liam, turns us toward the park. The compartment of the carriage is large enough to seat four, but Charlotte is pressed up against my side, my arm relaxed around her shoulders, and her small hand is resting on my thigh.

I took my jacket off before settling myself in the carriage, and I'm glad I did. The combination of the warm air and her hot body against mine has caused my own temperature to rise. Her fingers trace small circles on the inside of my thigh as her hand grazes softly back and forth just above my knee. We're quiet for a few minutes, just taking in the sites of the park as we enter. As we go further into the park, the world around us seems to grow still and I tilt my head back to look up at the sky.

I raise my hand and point up. "Look. You can actually see the stars." When you're in the city itself, it's so bright that seeing the night stars is difficult. Tonight, they light up the sky like diamonds against black silk.

"They're so beautiful," she breathes out as her head leans back against my arm.

My gaze has shifted from the sky to her, and I stare, mesmerized. "You're beautiful." I raise a hand and brush her locks away from her face, sweeping my thumb across her cheek. Her eyes have swung from the sky to lock with mine. "And I want to kiss you so, so badly right now, but I'm keeping that promise I made in the car."

"Oh..." Her pink tongue darts out against one corner of her mouth, dragging the edge of her upper lip back, before she captures it in her teeth. She releases it when my eyes move to her mouth, and she purses her lips tightly in response then speaks. "I think sometimes it's okay for someone to break their promises."

I chuckle lightly and take the bait. "Oh, really?"

She nods her head and scoots closer to me. "Especially if no one is hurt by the broken promise." She lifts her shoulders in a small shrug. "Kinda like a white lie."

I shift my body and bring my other hand to her face as I lower my lips close to hers. "I can't promise that you won't get hurt."

"Sometimes, a little pain is good, too. Makes you stronger." Her voice is barely a whisper now.

"Okay, but don't forget you asked for it." And then I sink the final inch and fuse my mouth to hers, my hand sliding around the back of her head to hold her close. She raises both her hands and snakes them around my neck, one hand threading through my short hair. Our kiss turns deeper, our bodies beginning to tangle around each other as we both succumb to the desire that's been building between us all week long.

My cock is a roaring ache between my legs that she keeps bumping as she presses against me, making it almost impossible for me to pull away from her, but I do, breathing heavily, my heart pounding in my chest. "Let's go back to your place, okay?"

"Okay." She pants, her small fingers scraping her messy hair away from her flushed cheeks.

"Liam, can you bring us back please?" I call over the horse's hooves hitting the cement.

"No problem. I'll turn around." He shouts back over his shoulder.

We somehow manage to keep our hands off each other for the fifteen-minute ride back to the park entrance, distracting our lust by pointing out places we've been to in the park before. We make a promise to come back again soon, but during the day, so we can go to the zoo together. Another place neither of us has visited in the city yet. I've already called for an Uber and pay Liam as we wait for it to arrive.

I watch as Charlotte strokes the long neck of the horse, cooing to it softly, thanking it for the ride, and I smile at her gentle nature. It's mind-boggling, in all the right ways, that one minute she's as aggressive and strong as a panther, and then in the next, as docile as a kitten. It's the perfect combination. She turns, looking for me, and smiles brightly when she sees me watching her.

"I know, I'm weird. I talk to them like they actually understand me." She gives the horse a final stroke and strolls over to me.

"It's sweet, not weird." I bend down and place a kiss on the top of her forehead. "It makes you more irresistible than you already are."

A white car slides up to the curb and honks, and we know it's our Uber driver. We get in the car and hold hands but remain silent. My thumb grazes back and forth against the soft center of her palm in anticipation of what's to come. Traffic is light and we arrive at her place in less than ten minutes.

We're out of the car and up the flight of stairs to her apartment in less than two minutes. She fishes around in her clutch and pulls out a set of keys, sliding one into the lock, then turns it free to push open the door. I follow behind her, and as soon as we're through, she drops what she's holding and twists around to face me. She takes one step before I spin her around and raise her arms, pinning her to the door.

"No stopping now," I warn as I lean down and crash my lips against hers.

~Charlotte~

I try to lower my arms but he pushes back against them, trapping me in place, and I swear, my arousal level just went through the roof. I whimper against his mouth, frustrated that I can't feel him. I want my hands on his skin, in his hair, around his cock. He chuckles against my mouth, sensing my frustration, and moves to nip the tender spot under my ear.

"This time, we're going to do things my way," he growls against my lobe, sucking it into his mouth, then swiping his tongue against it, my back arching away from the door and pushing my stomach into his hard length.

"I don't care how we do it, Trey, just fucking do it!" I plead, trying to capture his mouth with mine, wanting to feel it back on mine. He consents and crushes his lips back against mine, finally releasing my hands, sliding his own down my body. He caresses every inch of me along the way, landing on my hips and pushing me back hard against the door. His lips leave mine and start a hungry trail down my neck to the top of my dress.

His hands have somehow inched their way up to meet where his lips are, and he grasps the edge of the material on each side of my breasts and pulls it down exposing me from the waist up. His lips follow the direction of the material, stopping when he reaches one of my swollen peaks. He blows a hot breath against the tip and then swipes his tongue slowly back and forth over the nipple.

I mewl, arching my back off the door, trying to push it further into his mouth. To my delight, he complies, wrapping his lips around the bud and then sucking hard. My hands land on his head, and I rake my fingers through his hair as he continues to suck, a bolt of lightning shooting straight down to my pussy causing it to tingle.

One hand releases my hip and slides down and under the material of my skirt, skimming across my thigh until it lands on the juncture between my legs. His mouth releases my breast, but only long enough to move to the other, and then devotes the same attention he gave the other. At the same exact time, he takes his hand and slides it underneath the thin strip I have covering my pussy and presses two fingers against my quivering bundle of nerves, wrenching a gasp from me.

My knees buckle under me as I call out to God, and I tighten my grasp on his head as I struggle to hold myself up. He continues to slide his fingers back and forth against my center but releases his hold on my nipple, trailing his lips back up to crash against mine again. I'm grinding myself down on his hand and clutching onto his shirt with both hands in an attempt to relieve some of the ache that's been building in me for hours, when he shoves me back against the door and steps back.

His lips are swollen as heavy breaths roll out from between them, a feral look in his eye. "Stay like that for just a minute."

My hands are at my sides, my chest heaving, my dress hanging from my waist as I nod my head in compliance. He shrugs his jacket off his shoulders and lets it drop to the floor, moving his fingers immediately to the buttons on his shirt to release the top three. He pulls the bottom out of his pants and then yanks the shirt over his head.

Just like before, I gasp in awe at his toned form. I move to take a step toward him, my body moving of its accord, wanting to touch him, wanting to help him undress, but he shakes his head.

"Stay there." He waits until I've stopped moving and then toes his shoes off, pushing them away from his body. Then he releases the buckle on his pants, pulling a condom out of the front pocket, before unfastening the clasp at his waist and pushing them off his body onto the floor. He steps out of them, wearing a pair of fitted boxers, his hard arousal straining against the cotton material, and stalks back to me.

He presses his body up against mine, shoving me back until I bump up against the door again. He slides his hands around my ass and lifts. "Wrap your legs around me." Then he clamps his lips over mine again, thrusting his length up against my spread core.

My mouth opens as a long moan escapes at the pleasure. He tightens his grip on my ass and then moves away from the door, carrying me over to the couch where he lays me down. He puts the condom between his teeth and then uses his hands to push his boxers off, his cock springing up hard and straight. My mouth waters at the sight of it, remembering what it felt like inside of me, and I move toward it.

He shakes his head and cups my cheek, stopping me before I can reach him, grabbing the condom out between his teeth with his other hand. "If you do that, I'll come in two seconds."

"But—"

"It's only nine-thirty, Charlotte. You've got all night. I'm not going anywhere." His voice is husky as he informs me he won't be leaving anytime soon, and another wave of electricity jolts me to my core. "Besides, I've been looking forward to this all night."

Before I can ask him what, he kneels on the floor between my legs and stares at his target. My pussy convulses at the mere thought of him going there, and I lean back as he moves forward. His hands move up to my dress and he tugs it, pulling it down and off of me, leaving only the black thong as my last scrap of clothing. Scrap is definitely the correct word to use in describing them. My lips have become so swollen that they aren't even covered by the fabric anymore.

Instead of removing them though, he lifts my leg and kisses my ankle, stroking a hand over the tied satin. "Do you know how fucking sexy these shoes are?"

I do know they're sexy. It's why I chose them tonight, and I'm so glad I did now. I nod my head, capturing my lip between my teeth.

"And I'm glad they're comfortable, 'cause when I'm done here, I'm going to fuck you in them. From behind."

Holy Mother of God. A wave of heat washes over me and my pussy throbs, a gasp of surprise coming me.

"I haven't even started yet, Charlotte." He smirks, lowering my leg as his moves his fingers upward between my thighs, stopping when he brushes up against my underwear. "I'm not really sure what purpose these serve." He glances up at me, sliding his fingers under the material against my hip, and then pulls them off. "Next time, just go without." He gives me another salacious grin. "Think of the time we could save."

"I'll take that into consideration," I pant out, watching as he moves his torso between my legs now, a wicked gleam in his eye as he lowers his lips to the inside of my thigh and begins kissing, nibbling, and licking his way toward my center.

I fall back against the couch the moment I feel his tongue graze against my nerves and clutch the cushion of the couch in one hand, while the other moves to my nipple and rolls it between my fingers. When he runs his entire tongue over my wetness, pushing my thighs open wider with his hands as he does, I twist my nipple harder, enjoying the dual sensation I get.

I let out a low 'O' of pleasure as he moves to slide not one, but two fingers easily into me and sucks my clit at the same time. My hips move naturally and begin to rock against his tongue as it moves back and forth against me, his fingers continuing to pump in and out of me.

"Oh my God, Trey... Feels so good..." seems to be my mantra as the same two phrases keep falling from my lips. I feel my orgasm climb higher and higher until he latches onto my clit and bites down, sucking hard, sending me toppling over the cliff, flying through the air, floating as I scream out my release, my pussy gripping around his fingers.

Before I can even catch my breath, he's moved up my body and sealed his mouth over mine in a wet kiss. It lasts only seconds before he breaks away and pulls me up. I grasp onto his arms, eager to feel him against me, but he spins me around and leans me over the back of the couch, moving his body against mine. I arch my back up into him, my body ready for anything more he wants to give me.

I hear the rip of foil, and then his body is gone from mine for a second before his arm snakes around my waist and he's over me again. His lips are on my shoulder, my back, and then at the crest of my ass. His hands grab onto both sides of my backside, and I feel his nose slide down my cheek and then his tongue as it licks all the way up my center. "You taste so fucking good, Charlotte," vibrates between my legs, and I have to force myself not to squeeze them together from the sensation. He drags his tongue over me one more time then rises up, holding his body over mine as he lines his cock up to my pussy. He rubs it back and forth across the wet opening and then slowly pushes inside of me.

My back arches low as I push back into him, ready for his size this time but still needing time to adjust to it. He reaches around with both hands and grabs my breasts, pinching the nipples between his fingers. My pussy immediately contracts, pulling him in deeper, and he groans, shoving forward, his entire cock now buried completely inside me.

"Ohhh, God…" I moan when he begins to slide slowly out and then shifts and rocks back into me hard. "Yes!" I cry, shoving back into him, wanting more. Wanting it harder. Wanting it faster.

"Do you like this, Charlotte? Do you like when I fuck you hard like this?" He surges his hips hard against my ass and I cry out my approval again.

"Yes! Yes! Yes! Feels so good!" I'm clawing at the material on the back of the couch, trying to tighten my grip as he crashes into me from behind, my ecstasy only increasing. I don't think it's possible for me to reach a higher nirvana until I feel a hard smack against my ass. I cry out from the pain but surprise myself when I look back, hoping for more.

Trey's fingers are digging into my ass, his eyes dark with lust as he meets my eyes. "Again?"

I nod my head vigorously, my hair swishing around my face, and bite my lip.

"Say it." He thrusts into me hard, my shoes slipping against the floor. "Tell me you want it."

"Hit me. I like when you smack me. Do it again." I'm practically begging, but I don't care. It felt so good when his hand left my ass, the sting traveling down my cheek and right to my core.

His hand swings up and comes down in a loud thwack, my head falling forward between my arms as I mewl out in pleasure. "God, yes. Please, again."

"Sweet Jesus, Charlotte, you're fucking incredible." He pants and then smacks me again, even louder this time, and I groan low as I thrust my ass back, increasing the tempo.

"Fuck me hard, Trey, now!" I yell, feeling another orgasm starting to take hold. His grip on my hips tightens and he pounds into me, his pelvis slamming into my ass with each thrust. I feel myself clench around his cock in one long grip, sparks igniting under my lashes as the world spins around me and I scream in relief.

"Fuck, yes!" I feel his cock begin to throb as his release takes him over the edge right behind me, his arms sliding around my waist to hold me tight as we both crash against the couch.

I can feel his heart thudding against his chest as he lays against my back, and I let out a long slow breath as I try to slow my own raging heart. He shifts slightly around me, triggering a small spasm in my pussy, and I whimper at the feeling. His cock jerks inside of me once in reaction and then he slides it slowly out of me, rising up off of me.

I just lay there for a minute, waiting for my body to come down from the high it's still on. I hear him moving around, a door opening, and then he's back at my side, slipping his hands under me and then lifting. His lips are against my cheek and he kisses me lightly. I slide my arms around his neck and nuzzle into him.

He carries me into my bedroom, the covers already pulled back, and lays me gently on top. He unties my shoes, drops each one to the floor, and then bends to kiss me again. "I'll be right back." And he is, in just a minute, and he gently wipes me with a warm washcloth then kisses me again. "Do you need anything?"

I roll over onto my back and smile up at him. "I need to pee, but I feel like rubber right now." I giggle and throw a hand over my face. "What have you done to me?"

He leans over me and places soft kisses on my cheek between my fingers. "I think it's called fucking you boneless."

"I think I like it," I whisper back shyly.

"I know I did," he says, his lips against mine as he does, then he kisses me. Long and deep and more sweetly than I can ever remember being kissed.

I do get up then and use the bathroom quickly. I return to the bedroom to find him sitting on the edge of the bed, boxers back on. I look at him curiously. "What is it?"

He lifts his shoulders and gives me a small smile. "I didn't know if I should stay? If you wanted me to?"

I climb back into the bed, still naked, and look at him. "You better. I think you promised me all night long."

He grins wickedly at me and then dives onto the bed, pulling me down with him, kissing me as we fall.

CHAPTER FOURTEEN

~Trey~

I shoot to a sitting position, pulled from a deep sleep, my eyes flying open, trying to figure out what's woken me up.

"Shhh, lay back down." Charlotte's voice floats dreamily up from under the covers, and I suddenly remember, I'm not at home. I'm still at her place, still naked, still fucking hard as a rock apparently, as I feel the wet trace of her tongue slide up my length.

"Ahhh," I groan out, following her instructions to lie back, heat encompassing my dick as she sucks it into her mouth. I close my eyes as my hand blindly finds the top of her head over the covers, holding it as she drags her mouth up and down my length.

I honestly didn't think it was possible to be this hard again after the three times we had sex during the night, but she's blowing that theory to hell. Literally. I groan loudly when her fingers start to stroke the underside of my balls and find myself thrusting deeper into her throat. She hums, swallowing my cock even further, my ass surging off the bed from the sensation.

My grip tightens as I feel my balls start to do the same and I try to lift her off me. "I'm going to come." I pant, trying to keep my hips on the bed as she continues to suck hard, and instead of stopping, pushes my hand away. "Fuuuuccckkk," I groan out.

I drive my head back into the pillow and dig my heels into the mattress as my cock swells and then explodes, warm cum sliding down her throat as she continues to swallow around me. "Sweet—Fucking—Jesus!" I roar as my fingers slide under the covers to clutch her hair, pulling it into my balled fists as my cock pulses out its release, every muscle in my body contracting.

My body jerks as she relaxes the suction on my length, a small pop sounding as I fall out of her mouth. She crawls up my body, her silky tresses emerging from under the covers, her lips puffy and pink and turned up devilishly at the corners. "Good morning."

"Morning," I drawl out, still recovering from her attention.

She comes to rest on my chest, her fingers skimming my shoulders as she leans down to brush a light kiss across my lips. "Aren't you glad you stayed?"

I chuckle and press my mouth against hers, worshipping the very lips that just ravished me to bliss. "So glad."

"Are you hungry?" She trails a finger across my chin as my eyebrow crooks up, a smirk playing across her mouth. "For food!" She slides her hand down my body and rests it on my now soft cock. "I think he's done for a bit."

I snatch her hand off my junk and drag it up, trapping it between our bodies. "Well, there are other methods, as you've just so effectively demonstrated."

She blushes. "Maybe later. I'm starving."

I shove my body up and roll over on top of her, trapping her underneath me, her eyes wide as she looks up at me. I lower my lips against hers and kiss lightly then push up and off her. "You cooking?"

She lets out a laugh, shaking her head. "Um, no. Sorry." She sits up on the bed and pulls the sheet around her body. "I can probably make you a really good bloody Mary, but that's about it. Cooking is not in my wheelhouse."

"I can cook," I offer. "Pretty well actually."

"Good to know." She taps her head to indicate she's storing that tidbit of information away. "Unfortunately, there isn't much in my fridge. Unless you want yogurt?"

"Get dressed." I walk to the side of the bed and wrap an arm around her, hauling her off the bed and up against my body. "I'll take you to breakfast."

"I thought you'd never ask," she responds, a triumphant smile gracing her face. "Actually, I'm going to take a quick shower first." She looks at me and pulls her lips back from her teeth. "I'm just a little bit dirty."

"Okay, but only if I can join you…"

A half hour later, I watch as she pulls on a pair of faded dungaree shorts, sans underwear, then looks over at me, a sexy smile appearing. "As requested." She then pulls a faded New England Patriots t-shirt over her head. Her nipples poke at the thin material of the shirt, causing a dull ache to throb below my waist, shocking even me at this point. This girl has my head fucking spinning. I try to focus on something else so ask about the shirt.

"The Patriots? Really? You're going to wear that walking around here?"

She shrugs. "Tom Brady is hot." Then she gives me a playful smile. "I lived there for a few years. That's where I went to nursing school."

"Ah," I reply. "Sundays should get interesting around here then. I'm an Eagles fan baby. Tried and true."

"You know what they say about a good fight, right?" She raises her brows seductively and strolls over to me. "Enhances the libido." She reaches me and places one finger on my chest, trailing it slowly down and around my nipple, then back up, under my chin to lift my lips to her waiting ones. A giggle erupts around her mouth as she latches on for a quick second then releases me, backing up a step.

"You're a fucking wildcat, baby. I love it." I stand and thread my fingers through her damp, wavy locks, pulling her back up against me, loving the feel of her little frame against mine, and kiss her breathless. This time, it's she who seems flustered when I pull away, which leaves me finally feeling like I've achieved a small victory.

"Still hungry?" I tease, seeing the buds of her nipples even more pronounced under her t-shirt.

She nods. "I feel bad though."

I frown. "Why?"

"I'm all comfy and you're stuck with your outfit from last night."

I look down and then slide my hands in my pockets. "It's an easy fix."

"Really?"

"Let's grab an Uber to my place. I'll change really quick and then we can grab breakfast at a joint near my place I like."

She bops her head. "Perfect."

~Charlotte~

We hop out of the Uber and I follow Trey to his building. He greets the doorman with a familiar nod and then ushers me inside to the elevator. We ride up eight floors, his hand holding mine, and then exit when the doors slide open.

"It's this way." He points to the right and we walk in that direction. He stops in front of 8C, pulling a set of keys from his jacket pocket to unlock the door, but pauses before he opens the door.

"I'm just going to apologize ahead of time for Trick. And if the apartment is a mess." He laughs nervously and then bumps the door open.

"Hey, asshole. Guess you got laid aga—" Trick's comment dies on his lips when he notices me, his gaze sweeping apologetically up to Trey's. "Sorry."

"You're such a dick." Trey cuffs him in the head as he strides by. "Be nice to her for five minutes while I change please."

"You need to call Cory, man," Trick yells as Trey walks into his bedroom. "She's fucking pissed!"

My heart lurches when I hear the part where Cory is a 'she'. *Is Trey seeing someone else? And why is she pissed?* Not that I have any official claim on him, but if we're going to be sleeping together, I guess I'll need to find out.

I'm still standing by the doorway, unsure where I should go, when Trick surprises me and gives me a half smile. "You want a cup of coffee? You look like maybe you do?"

I nod gratefully. "God, yes."

"Come on." He waves for me to follow him, so I do. As he walks past the long, solid white marble breakfast bar, he pulls out a stool and pats the seat. "Make yourself comfortable."

I pull myself up onto the stool and watch as he grabs a cup down from an exposed shelf and then places it in the Keurig machine. He pops a pod in the machine and then presses a button.

I'm engrossed in the Celtic type lettering he has tattooed across his back, "*All Pain Is Fleeting,*' and the meaning it may have behind it when he turns back around. "How do you like it?"

"Do you have any cream?"

"It's flavored. Hazelnut I think." He walks over to the double-door stainless steel fridge then pulls out a container. "This okay?"

"That's great." I watch as he moves back to the counter to take a spoon out of a drawer. He's wearing only a pair of long cotton shorts, so it's hard not to notice how fit and good looking he is. I can see the appeal Gabby would have for him. Seeing him up close like this, I would guess he's a few years older than Trey. He's at least as tall but broader in the shoulders and a little bit more muscular. And where Trey's chest is almost bare, Trick's is scattered with dark, curly hair across his pecs. I pause, my eyes locking onto the thick, metal ring in one nipple, and blush when he notices me looking at him.

One corner of his mouth cocks up, wondering I'm sure, about what I'm thinking, but he doesn't say a thing. I do instead, trying to appear casual but probably failing miserably because I can hear the nervous shake to my voice. "What's your tattoo mean?"

He brings his eyes up to mine and squints as he stares at me. His fists clench and then open wide as a strange sort-of smile appears on his face. "I guess it just means that pain only hurts as long as you let it."

Before I can ask another question, he places the coffee in front of me. "You need anything else? I have somewhere I need to be."

"Uh, no. Thank you," I say as he breezes back around the bar, a door shutting quietly a second later. I take a sip of the hot coffee and think to myself, *that's what is referred to as dark, broody and mysterious*, laughing softly to quell my nerves.

I jump when I feel a pair of hands latch onto my waist from behind, and then immediately relax when Trey's nose nuzzles against my neck. "Can I have a sip of that coffee?" He spins my chair around slowly and slips the mug from my hands, inhaling a small sip, then humming in delight. "That's so good."

I nod. "Trick made it." I sweep my gaze appreciatively over the fitted light-blue t-shirt he's wearing with a pair of khaki cargo shorts.

His brows jump up. "Really?" He purses his lips. "Wonders never cease I guess."

He sets the coffee on the counter and lifts me off the stool. "Come on! Let's go. I'm starving!"

A little over an hour later, we're standing in front of the entrance to the Central Park Zoo, and I'm hopping in a place like an excited child. "You're sure you want to do this? I mean, I know we talked about it last night, but I didn't mean today!"

"I'm positive." He waves his arms over his head at the sky. "It's a beautiful day. Besides, it's the middle of August and I haven't really spent any time outside yet this summer."

"Yay!" I clap my hands and then throw them around him in a hug, dropping a happy kiss against his lips.

He chuckles, gripping his hands around my waist as he lowers me. "If going to the zoo makes you smile like this, we can do it every weekend."

Ohhhh... I like the sound of that. I'm sure I'm blushing. In fact, I know I am because I can feel my cheeks heating. The fact that he wants to spend more weekends with me in the future has my heart beating double-time in excitement. I turn away from him and grab his hand, pulling him to the entrance. "Let's go then!"

He buys two tickets and plucks a map off the counter as we enter to sounds of children yelling, parents calling out, and birds chirping throughout the trees. He pulls the map open and we begin walking, exploring each one of the exhibits as we go. We wander through the tropic zone, cooing at the gorgeous birds while I shiver in fear at some of the dangerous snakes kept there. Trey completely surprises me when he wants to stay and watch the turtles for more than half an hour. He says he loves how simple and serene they are, so different from some of the moments his everyday life consists of.

When we reach the large cat sanctuary, I'm completely awestruck by the lithe and grace of some of the animals we watch. Trey pulls me to an enclosure I haven't looked in yet and positions me in front of the bars.

"See that?" He points to what looks like a smaller version of a leopard but is much lighter in color, close to a dusty gray but a shy too dark to be called white. "She reminds me of you," he whispers in my ear, his arms wrapped around my shoulders, dangling in front of me.

I tilt my head back to look at him, a curious smile on my face. "Me? Why?"

"Well, besides the obvious, she's beautiful. Petite, graceful, almost ghost like in how she moves." He points to her again. "Watch how she jumps to that rock."

I do, noticing the strength in her hind legs when she pushes off, then how nimbly she lands on her paws.

"See how strong she is? That fierceness in her eyes? That's how I see you."

I watch the snow leopard for a second, trying to see everything in her that he sees in me, and then spin around in his arms. "You're comparing me to another pussy?" I joke, intimidated by the feelings he's stirring in me and wanting to try and make light of the moment.

He chuffs and then leans his forehead against mine. "I'm comparing you to the elegance and strength I see in her."

"Trey—" I'm stunned by his observation of me. To believe he sees me as a creature so regal and powerful. So enchanting. "I'm not sure I'm all that you described."

He leans forward and presses his lips to mine softly. "You are. And so much more."

My pulse quickens as he pushes me back against the exhibit and wraps his hands around the bars, caging me in, trapping me like the cat behind me. He grazes his nose over mine and then nips my lips before covering them, sweeping his tongue across, nudging me to open my mouth. I comply, his kiss like a spark igniting gas-infused kindling, my body bursting into flames. He drives his body against mine, every inch of him flush against me, his arousal hard against my stomach.

His hands move to my face as he tears his lips from mine. "I can't seem to get enough of you." His voice is hoarse and full of need.

"The feeling is mutual," I murmur back against his lips, nipping at them.

We hear a loud clearing of the throat from behind us, and then someone muttering, "Kids present."

Trey releases his hold on me and steps back quickly, shifting his bulge discreetly as he pulls down the hem of his t-shirt. "Sorry," he states and then grabs my hand, pulling me quickly away. I barely have time to see the large grizzly bears as he rushes past, taking me in the direction of a small building.

"Thank fuck," is all I hear before he pushes a door open, pulling me inside the family bathroom unit and slamming the door behind me before thrusting my back against it with his body, turning the lock as he does. "I can't take another minute knowing you've got nothing on underneath your shorts." His fingers work the snap and zipper on the offending garment, forcing them down off my legs.

I fumble with the button on his shorts as his lips claim mine in a brutal kiss, his fingers now moving against my core, finding me wet and more than willing. I finally get the button free and slide my hand inside to find he's commando as well, a grin forming around my lips as he continues to kiss me.

He moves his mouth to my neck, nipping it with his teeth and then latching on, sucking the little bite marks I'm sure he's left. His hands reach up under my legs and hoist me up, pressing his center against me.

We haven't said a single thing. Small pants and grunts sound from us as we move and adjust to each other, my legs gripping him tightly as he slips a hand between us and lines his cock up to my opening. He surges his hips forward, his length sliding to the hilt in one thrust.

"Ooooh fuck!" He stills and brings his face to mine. "I'm not wearing a condom."

I shake my head quickly back and forth, the feeling of him bare inside of me pure bliss. "I'm on the pill. Don't you dare fucking stop."

His mouth crashes back against mine, his hips slamming me up against the door as he begins thrusting deep inside of me relentlessly. My arms grip his shoulders mercilessly, my pussy clenching around him just as tightly.

"So. Fucking. Amazing." He pants in my ear each time he rams inside of me, each time harder than before. And I love it. I feel my orgasm begin to build, and in two short thrusts, I combust, my teeth sinking into the fabric of his t-shirt to try and muffle the loud moan that I cry out.

One hand slams against the door behind me as he drills forcefully into me three more times, my pussy convulsing madly around him when I feel hot, warm jets suddenly pumping into me. My pussy clenches around his cock, trying to drain every ounce of him inside of me, reveling in this feeling. This unkempt desire he has for me. I've never let a man come inside me before, and this knowledge alone has my head spinning.

I release the grip my mouth has on his shoulder as he slides out of me, lowering me to my feet before he steps back. His face is flushed and his breaths are coming out in short, quick gasps. "Sweet Jesus. What the fuck are you doing to me?" He steps against me, crushing his mouth to mine as he cradles my face, smothering out any reply I may have.

We clean up quickly, giggling, knowing how naughty what we just did was, and then slip discreetly out of the restroom, keeping our heads low as we slink by waiting people. *I just had dirty bathroom sex in a public place! Best Saturday afternoon ever.*

He grabs my hand in his and leads me down a small slope to the exit of the zoo. I think we're definitely done here today. As we're about to exit, I see something in the shop window and yank his arm, pulling him to a stop. "Give me a minute?"

"Sure." He points to a vendor stand a few feet away. "Want something to drink?"

I nod my head. "Water please."

I find him a few minutes later outside the store, gift bag in my hand, grinning like the Cheshire cat. He points to the bag as he hands me a bottled water, the cap already loosened for me. "Whatcha got there?"

"I'll give it to you later." I take a drink as he arches a brow and gives me a curious look but doesn't press further as we stroll out of the zoo and back toward the street. I'm about to ask him what he wants to do next when I see him raise his arm to flag down a taxi. Then he looks over at me, his lips turned down slightly.

"I hate to end this perfect afternoon, but I've got a commitment tonight and have to go do a few things beforehand."

I'm sure he sees the disappointment in my face as I try to hide it behind a forced smile. "Oh, okay, sure."

A taxi pulls up beside me, and he opens the back door as he locks his gaze to mine. "Last night? Today?" He leans forward and presses a long kiss to my lips. "The absolute best time I can remember having in forever."

Well, that makes me feel a little better. "Me too," I whisper back.

"Call you tomorrow?" he asks as I slide into the taxi.

I frown and shake my head. "I'm working the next four days."

"Then I'll see you Monday when I'm on again," he states before handing a twenty to the driver and giving him my address then looks back at me. "I'll miss you."

"Oh!" That reminds me of the gift I got him. I lift the bag and place it in his hands. "Maybe this will help." Then I pull the door shut and blow him a kiss. He looks down at the bag for a second, then flashes me a gorgeous smile and waves as we pull away.

CHAPTER FIFTEEN

~Trey~

I watch until the taxi merges into traffic and then open the bag she gave me, a huge smile forming when I see what's inside. I pull it out and hold it up, the black and gray dots on the white fur of the stuffed snow leopard sparkling a little in the sunlight. "My own little leopard," I mumble, sliding it back into the bag. I love it. Almost as much as I love spending time with her.

I scratch my chin as I realize the word love is rolling around in my thoughts quite a bit. My heart jumps a few extra beats as this flash epiphany screeches into awareness and I curse under my breath. I'm developing serious feelings for this girl, and I just sent her away because I have to go on a 'date' with another one. This is seriously fucked up. I know I need to address it, but I have no idea where to start. I push the concern away for now and throw my hand up to hail another taxi. I don't feel like waiting for an Uber and need to get home.

Twenty minutes later, I walk into my building and up to the apartment. I haven't checked my phone in hours, and I'm not surprised that I have at least ten texts from Cory. I call out to see if Trick's home but don't get an answer. I sigh loudly and then hit Cory's number, knowing I'm in for an earful.

"Feeling better?" she states sarcastically, instead of hello, when she answers the phone.

"Hi to you, too, Cory."

"Don't you 'hi' me. I know you weren't sick yesterday." I hear her clicking on a keyboard as she continues to chastise me. "And then you don't answer a single text from me today, so I have *no* idea if you're going to meet your commitment for tonight. What the fuck, Trey?"

I open my mouth to explain, but she cuts me off. "This is not how we do business at Temptations. You got a problem? You need to tell me now." Her tone is curt and I know she's not going to put up with any of my bullshit excuses, so I just lay it on the line for her.

"I met a girl. I like her."

"And you kissed her?" she retorts, no humor in her voice. "I don't care, Trey. This is a job. We're a professional organization in which clients do not expect to be stood up. You made us look bad and I'm not going to put up with it. You want out? Just tell me and it's done."

Well, shit. Thanks for the support. "You know I need the job. Stop busting my goddamn balls! I've worked there for two years. Two! Have I ever called out sick before?"

"That's always true until the first time." A long sigh travels through the phone. "Listen, Trey, I get it. Trying to have a personal life when you're in this business isn't easy. So, you need to decide what you want and let me know, okay?"

"Yeah, I know." I nod, even though I know she can't see me. "I'm in, Cory. I need the money. I'll figure it out."

"Okay. So, you're good for tonight? It's Lillian Prescott, an easy one. She just wants an arm for a function she needs to attend this evening. Nice suit, not black tie."

"Yeah, I'm good. I got your email with the details."

"Gene will be there to pick you up at seven."

"Got it," I confirm.

"And, Trey?"

"Yeah?" I answer.

"Answer my fucking texts next time or I'll fire your ass." Then she hangs up.

I scoff out loud and toss my phone on the table in frustration. Part of me would love to get fired. Would love to be over at Charlotte's right now. Would love to spend another night with her in my arms, savoring the way she feels when she's curled like a kitten into my side. But the practical side of me, the one that knows I still owe thousands in school debt, blows out an exasperated breath as I head to the bathroom to shower and prepare for my appointment.

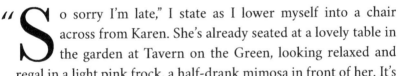

"So sorry I'm late," I state as I lower myself into a chair across from Karen. She's already seated at a lovely table in the garden at Tavern on the Green, looking relaxed and regal in a light pink frock, a half-drank mimosa in front of her. It's Sunday, and I'm ten minutes late for our eleven o'clock brunch date.

"Please!" She waves her hand dismissively. "I figured it was so you could build up the anticipation of our meeting." She winks playfully at me. "Besides, seeing the look on Jennifer Duncan's face when you sat down just made it all worth it!" She leans forward and speaks quietly, a teasing twinkle lighting up her eyes. "I'm sure I'll be the talk of the club by tomorrow afternoon!"

"You are such a minx! Always looking to stir the pot, aren't you?" I admonish playfully.

"When you're my age, dearest, you get your thrills where you can." She lets out a little hoot of laughter and reaches for her drink, taking a sip, then questioning me. "Late night?"

One side of my mouth lifts in a grin as I muse over the evening before. "You could say that."

The date with Lillian Prescott was more enjoyable than anticipated. It was over by eleven, with no requests for further 'benefits' from the date, much to my relief. Most of the women I escort are actually extremely attractive. And definitely rich. Rich enough to tempt even myself into crossing a line I don't. I'm okay with being an escort. I am. But I don't want to be a prostitute. I know it's was a thin line, but it makes me feel better to think I have limits and try to maintain some decency regarding how I think of myself.

When I got home last night and crawled into bed the night before, I sent a text to Charlotte wishing her goodnight. I wasn't even sure she'd still be awake but was thrilled when I got an immediate reply back from her. Within five minutes, we were facetiming each other, and another fifteen minutes after that, I was moaning my release as we had some of the hottest phone sex ever. Definitely a perfect ending to my day.

"Oooh, you look like you've been up to something naughty," she teases. "Tell me everything!"

I spend the next half-hour telling her about Charlotte. How Trick initially set me up as a favor to Gabby. How that night turned into something more than I could have ever expected, but that I walked away because it was just supposed to be a 'job'. Then I tell her how we ended up working together at the hospital and our time together up to the day we spent together yesterday. I tell her everything and then open up about my fear of telling her about my job at Temptations.

"Well, honey, it's not going to be easy, that's for sure!" she admonishes. "You should have told her that very same night you explained your name situation! Then you wouldn't be in this mess."

I fiddle with my fork, pushing the remnants of my food around on my plate. "I know. I'm screwed. I've waited too long and now I don't know how I'm supposed to tell her."

"You're just going to have to do it. I don't think there's an easy answer to this one, Trey." She clucks and then taps her finger on the table. "That is unless you'll finally relent and let me help you with those loans?"

"Nope." I chuckle at her persistence. "I pay my own way. You know that by know."

"I do, I do." She nods, turning her head back and forth. "Tell her soon. The longer you wait, the harder it's going to be."

~Charlotte~

As I walk next to Trey, I can't believe it's already been over a month since I bumped into him in this very hallway. This is our first shift on together in three days, and coincidentally, that many days since I've seen him. Just being next to him has my skin buzzing. Generally, our schedules mostly match, so I get to see him almost every shift that I work. If we have the same weekdays off, we usually spend them together. I'm close to the river, so we've been renting bikes and riding them along the trail there, and now that summer is shifting to fall, we spend hours walking through Central Park, learning where all the hidden corners are. The nights are mostly spent at my place since I'm roommate free. My fridge has never been so well stocked, and I swear, I've gained at least five pounds from the amazing breakfasts he always cooks for me on the nights he does stay.

Weekends are trickier for him. He said he picks up shifts working another job to help with his tuition, so it's a crap-shoot as to whether or not we spend time together on those days and nights. But, it's those nights, the nights he rings my door after hours, surprising me with his presence, my heart always soaring in delight, that are the best.

He's asked for my help with stitching up a patient with a bad laceration who won't sit still for him, so I'm surprised when he pushes through the door of the room he's led me to and it's empty.

The click of the lock on the door right before he yanks me into his arms quickly has me making sense of his little white lie.

"I've missed you so damn much the last few days." His chocolate eyes hold mine as he looks down at me, his hand snaking around my neck, the other clutching around my waist and holding me tight.

"Who knew three days could feel like thirty?" I murmur back, captivated by the hunger I see brewing under his lashes. "Can you stay at my place tonight?"

"Wild horses couldn't keep me away, babe." He dips his head, dropping a tender kiss to the tip of my nose, then brushes his lightly against it as he slides his lips over mine. I open my mouth in invitation, desperate for the taste of him after not having it the last three days, and moan when his tongue sweeps across mine. Every time I kiss him feels like the first all over again, the tempo of my pulse quickening as my heart begins to race, my body instantly growing warm.

I curl my fingers around the neck of his scrubs, using what little strength I have to swivel his body and push him down onto the hospital bed behind him. My mouth breaks from his as he falls back and I tell him to stay. His brows arch high as his mouth shoots up in a grin when I toe of my crocks and slide my bottoms off my legs.

He seems to understand where this is going, and I nod my approval when he shifts his hands to the tie on his scrub bottoms and pulls it undone. I stalk to the bed and crawl up between his legs, dragging my body over his hard length, positioning myself so I'm straddled over him. I reach my hands to his waist and wrench the fabric of his bottoms low enough for his cock to spring free and then tilt my hips back before shifting them forward to slide him inside me.

My head falls back in ecstasy as I lower myself slowly down his thick shaft, and then, once he's completely buried inside me, begin to glide my hips back and forth. A low, animalistic moan slips from my lips as my sensitive bud drags across his cock each time I grind against him.

"I guess you did miss me," he growls under me, his hands moving to my hips to help me rock against him harder. I lean forward, snaking my hands under the material of his shirt, tracing them up over the smooth grooves of his stomach until I reach his chest. I bring my mouth to his and capture his lower lip between my teeth and bite gently before swishing my tongue over and then inside his mouth. This changes the angle of my body and he takes advantage, his fingertips biting into the skin of my waist as he begins to thrust upward forcefully, my clit absorbing every bit of the pounding against it.

My jaw falls open as it forms a small O shape, a mewl like sound rising from my throat as I detonate, my pussy contracting and then convulsing around him before I feel his warm seed shoot up inside of me, a guttural sound vibrating from him as he continues to slam into me for another few pumps before gripping me tightly up against him.

I lay my head over his chest, his heart galloping against my cheek as we both catch our breath. His fingers slip under my shirt and trace lazily across my lower back. I want to lay here like this forever, his body under mine, his heart beating for me, but know we will be missed soon if we aren't already. I lift myself off his chest and then push my waist off his, severing the connection of our bodies as I step to the floor.

"Come back," he groans, reaching his hands out to me. "Want more."

I giggle as I reach for a towel in one of the cupboards to clean myself up. "Me too, but we have to get back to work." I slide my bottoms back up my legs and then my shoes on my feet. "We can pick up where we left off later tonight at my place, okay?"

I walk to the door and turn the lock, looking back one last time to blow him a kiss as I sneak out of the room, leaving him to get dressed. When I step out, Gabby's leaning against the opposite wall, a knowing smirk on her face. "You all done in there?" She points her finger to the door and waves it in a small circle.

I fidget with my badge, my cheeks blazing as I chew the inside of it and look sheepishly back at her. "I haven't seen him for a few days." I turn and begin moving down the hallway toward the charting area. "Okay?" I glance over at her. "Sorry."

"Hey, you don't have to apologize to me." She cackles salaciously under her breath. "I'd climb that tree every chance I got if it was in my yard, too."

I slap her lightly on her arm. "You are incorrigible, Gabrielle!" We've reached the nurses' station, which thankfully is quiet and I sit down on one of the chairs, her moving beside me to do the same.

She spins her chair so she's facing mine, her features turning serious. "Not to complain or anything, but since you've been shacking up with Mr. Sexy Pants, I never see you anymore." She sticks her bottom lip out in an exaggerated pout.

"Not to complain or anything, huh?" I mimic playfully and then provide her with a genuine smile. "Then let's do something. You have something in mind?"

She slides closer to me, a mischievous grin on her face. "There's an event at the Sapphire Resort in mid-town this weekend for that movie that's releasing. You know the one that has that guy in it you like?"

I raise my eyebrows and then my shoulders. "Need a little more than that to go on, Gabs."

She waves her hand around in the air. "You know, the blond guy. Hot. Was in that motorcycle show. Charlie something or other."

My eyes brighten in excitement as I realize who she's referring to. "Wait! Shut the front door! You have access to an event he's going to be at?" I mean, don't get me wrong, I'm all about Trey right now, but if I can get me a sighting in of this hot, sexy actor, I'm going for it.

"Well, Daddy does. And he put me on the guest list. For two."
She tilts her head as she grins wickedly. "You in?"

'Oh, I'm in." I shake my head up and down, a wide smile on my
own face.

"You don't gotta check first with you know who?" she asks,
referring to Trey of course.

"He's probably working anyway." I roll my eyes. "Fucking
second job."

Gabby's expression changes, her smile disappearing as she
snorts. "Yeah, that's one way to put it."

"Put what?" My hackles raise in suspicion.

"Nothing." She stands and grabs a chart off the stack on the
table. "I'm going to go do some patient checks."

My eyes narrow at her attempt to change the subject.

"It's nothing," she states firmly. "We're going shopping beforehand, by the way," she calls over her shoulder as she strides away
from me. "I'm gonna have you looking so hot, Charlie-what's-his-
name is gonna want your number!"

I chuckle as she disappears around the corner then turn my
focus to the charts I've been neglecting for a little too long.

CHAPTER SIXTEEN

~Trey~

I grumble as I stuff my leg into the dress pants I have laid on the bed, yanking them up over my hips before fastening the clasp. I haven't heard from Charlotte all day, and I'm missing her like hell. And to make matters worse, I'm getting ready for a date with Lucy Greene. She's the last person I want to spend time with tonight, but she always tips at least five hundred bucks. Mostly because she ends up making a fool out of herself every time we're together. She drinks too much and then will try to get me to fuck her. Which certainly ain't happening. But I need the extra money, especially since I've been taking less appointments lately, so here I am, getting dressed. I'd much rather spend my free time with Charlotte, but I've got a payment due on my tuition next week, and the sooner I can get it paid off, the sooner I can quit this job.

I slip a dark gray dress shirt over my shoulders, button it, then tuck it into my Tom Ford dress pants. I do actually like dressing up. Tonight, I'm putting on some of the best I have for the heavy hitter event Mrs. Greene has me escorting her to. It's one of the perks of working at Temptations. They'll cover seventy-five percent of any clothing we buy for our jobs. I damn straight couldn't afford a suit like this otherwise.

I finish dressing and then spritz a little cologne on. I chuckle, noting that I never wear the Aqua di Gio when I have date appointments anymore. I reserve that strictly for her. For Charlotte. I smile when I think of her running her nose against my neck, inhaling and then literally biting the tender skin as she tells me how delicious I smell when I've got it on. Nope, I don't want to share that with anyone else now. It's for her, and her only.

I know she's been out with Gabby all day shopping for an outing they have tonight, but I wish she would have picked up one of the phone calls I attempted to her today. I haven't seen her in two days, and now it's been almost twenty-four since I've spoken to her. I pause as I walk to the kitchen and think about that. Her absence is like a hole in my heart. *After only twenty-four hours. Fuck.* I'm falling for this girl. Lightning strikes. I've *already* fallen for this girl. So. Fucking. Hard.

I take a step and then stop again. *Well, shit. I didn't see that coming.* I rake a hand over my face as I cover the smile that's formed at my realization. *I think I'm in love with her.*

"What the fuck is that look on your face?" Trick is standing across the living room, also dressed in a suit, staring at me.

I blink and shrug my jacket into place. "Nothing," I say dismissively.

"Uh-huh," he replies, not an ounce of conviction that he's buying what I'm selling. "Who you got?"

"Mrs. Greene." I grimace and shrug. "You?"

"I don't know. Someone new. Carrie Michaels."

I walk by him and slap him on the shoulder as I head for the door. "Try to be nice."

"Yeah, and don't you have too much fun."

I grunt. "Not a chance."

Forty-five minutes later, Lucy Greene is sliding her hand into the crook of my elbow as I escort her down a long hallway leading to the ballroom we're headed for. "You look very handsome tonight, Maddox. Thank you for that." She's still sober, so I know she's being polite and not trying to get in my pants. Yet.

"I wouldn't be doing my job if I didn't, Lucy." I give her a playful wink and my most charming smile as we enter the huge room and merge into a throng of other well-dressed attendees.

"Oh, look!" She points to the bar. "I see Mary over there."

I smile politely, groaning inwardly at her attempt to get closer to the bar, knowing full well what her real intentions are. Sure enough, after a very quick hello to Mary, she sidles over to the bar and orders a vodka martini. *Let the shit show begin.* She turns to me coquettishly and asks if I'd like a drink. "Water, please."

I always order water, but she always asks what I want anyways. I can drink. I have a driver. But on certain appointments, I've learned it's better to keep a clear head. In Lucy's case, it's a must. She lifts the martini from the bar, shimmying herself back against me, then leads me through the mix of people.

"I'm sorry, Maddox." She takes a sip of the drink as we stroll. "I know I promised I wouldn't drink the next time you escorted me, but Daniel is supposed to be here tonight with his new little hussy." She takes another sip through seething lips. "He knows this is my side of town, and he decided to come anyway! And to bring that little tramp with him. I just need a little liquid courage in case I do see him, and you, of course, to make him jealous."

I place my hand over hers where it lays on my arm and squeeze gently, smiling down at her. "Then you'll show him, won't you?"

"You understand, don't you?" She smiles in relief as she drains the last of the martini. "I knew you would."

Oh boy, this is going to be a fun night. We reach the table we've been assigned to, and I pull out a chair for her and then sit down beside her. Before she's even set her clutch on the table, she flags down a passing waiter and orders another martini. Two martinis later, she's feeling the effects, and as such, now has her hand on my thigh as she talks animatedly to the other people at our table.

After dinner, dessert is served as a band begins to play music from a stage at the end of the room. They're playing old time classics, and my mind immediately roams to thoughts of Charlotte and dancing with her this summer under the tent. Mistaking the smile on my face as something more, Lucy rises wobbly from the table, sliding my hand into hers as she does, urging me to stand. "I'd like to dance."

It's the last fucking thing I want to do with her, but I don't have a choice. It's my job and it's what she's paying me for. And, really, it's dancing, not screwing, so I shouldn't mind. Two months ago, I wouldn't have had a second thought about it, but everything has definitely shifted for me. Of course, I can't refuse, so I smile and lead her toward the dance floor, wrapping my arm around her waist, lifting her other hand up near my shoulder as I begin to sway her in a circle.

She's tipsy, to say the least. It only takes two turns before her cheek is resting on my shoulder, her long blonde locks spilling down my chest. She lets out a heavy sigh as she leans against me, and I feel sad for her. Sad that she's so lonely and feels that this is the only way to try and fill a void in her life. I place a small kiss on the top of her forehead, feeling sorry that a beautiful woman like her has been reduced to this because of the actions of one man.

I let out my own sigh then and raise my head to glance around the dance floor, freezing when my gaze locks onto Charlotte. My initial response is to smile in joy. My heart literally jumps in my chest I'm so happy to see her. And fucking hell. She looks insanely gorgeous. She's wearing some kind of red silk wrapped around her body like a glove, her lips painted the same exact shade. She's stunning. My cock stirs in my pants just at the sight of her.

But then, then I see the look on her face. The furrowed brow, her mouth open wide, her eyes even wider as she stares at me across the space dividing us. I release Lucy and push her back from me. "Can you—" I reach my hand out to steady her when I see her sway. "Will you excuse me for just a moment?" I release her and wait one second to make sure she doesn't fall over. "Will you be okay?"

She nods slowly, her reflexes like molasses from all the alcohol she's consumed. "I'll be fine."

I nod abruptly and then stride away. A stricken Charlotte, still frozen in place, continues to stare at me until I reach her.

She opens her mouth. Closes it. Looks over toward the dance floor and then back at me. "What the fuck is going on, Trey? Who the hell is that woman?"

I place a hand on her arm, but she shakes it off. "Don't you dare touch me right now." She stomps her beautifully soled foot. "Not until I know what the hell is going on. I thought you were working."

"I am, but—" Before I can continue, she interrupts me.

"Is that Cory?" Then she shakes her head as she absorbs what I said a second ago. "Wait, what?"

I rear back in shock at the same time. *How the hell does she know about Cory?* I rake a hand through my hair then groan when I see Gabby walking up behind Charlotte. "Charlie?" Gabby's eyes shift in my direction, a look of surprise on her face. "Trey? What are you doing here?"

I'm about to answer when I feel a hand slide up my arm and grasp on, pulling me in the other direction. "Maddox, honey, are you going to introduce me to your friends?"

Charlotte's eyes blaze with fury as they dart back and forth from me to Lucy, her cheeks turning almost the same shade as her dress. "Yes, why don't you introduce us, *Maddox?*" There's no mistaking the marked enunciation of my name as she spits it out.

I gently extricate Lucy's fingers from my arm and take a step closer to Charlotte. My heart is beating so hard I feel like it's going to rip through my chest. I lower my voice so that only she can hear me. "I know this looks bad, but I swear I can explain. Please. Let me take her home and I'll meet you back at your place."

She looks at me like she wants to claw my goddamn eyes out. I can see that her mind is spinning, her tiny hands clenched into tight fists, her pulse beating so hard I can see it throbbing from the vein on her neck.

"*Please*," I beg. "Give me a chance to explain."

"Fine," she seethes out between clenched teeth, and then spins on her heel, grabbing Gabby's hand as she does, and stomps off through the crowd.

~Charlotte~

I grab Gabby's hand and pull her with me as I storm away from Trey. I feel like I'm going to throw up and aim for the bathrooms I see across the hall when we walk out of the ballroom. I push through the door and then fall to my knees in front of the toilet, a sob escaping me. I clutch the side of the seat and dry heave, my stomach lurching when I close my eyes and see that woman draped on Trey as they danced.

A hand lightly touches my back as fingers pull my hair back away from my face. "You okay? What can I do?" Gabby's soft voice carries over my shoulder.

I let out a shorty cry and shake my head, wiping my nose with the back of my arm. "Who the fuck was that, Gabby?" I push myself up off the floor and turn to her. "And why the hell is she calling him Maddox?" I walk past her and go to the sink, turning the cold water on. "Is that Cory?"

"How do you know about Cory?" she replies, my hand freezing under the water as I'm about to scoop some into my mouth. I look up and find her in the reflection of the mirror.

"How do *you* know about Cory?" I ask. My stomach rolls again at the thought that my own best friend might be keeping a secret from me as I watch her shift nervously in place.

"I think you should let Trey explain," she replies quietly.

I shake the water from my hand and then spin around, my temper flaring. "Oh, no! You are not going to choose this moment in time to finally be quiet. I am your best friend. You are going to tell me right now what the hell is going on!"

I'm standing directly in front of her, my finger shaking as I point it at her. "Has he been with someone else this whole time? And you knew it?" My voice trembles at the very thought that both of them may have betrayed me.

She shakes her head vigorously. "No!" Then she takes my hand, lowering it to grasp it in hers. "It's not like that, Charlie. I swear."

"Then what is it!" I demand, close to tears. "Tell me!"

"She's not his girlfriend. Cory is his manager," she states matter-of-factly, not making anything clearer to me.

"What? What are you talking about?" I pull my hand from hers and pace back and forth before her, trying to make sense of everything.

Gabby lets out a really long breath and then speaks. "Trey is a professional escort."

I stop mid-step, dropping my foot to the floor, and then swivel to face her. "What?"

She lifts her shoulders once. "He works for an escort agency. People hire him to accompany them places." She shrugs again like it's no big deal.

"He's a prostitute?" I yell. Then, just as quickly, another thought rips into consciousness. "And you knew!" I stomp over to her and jab my finger against her chest when I see the telling answer on her face. "You fucking knew and you didn't tell me?" She looks at me, fear in her eyes, not answering. I'm about to spin away in disgust when another bolt of realization sears through my body, this one hurting the most, because I know what the answer's going to be before I even ask it. I lift my eyes to her and ask it anyway. "You hired him, didn't you? That night of your dad's party. You hired him to seduce me."

Her face says it all. I step back as if I'd been slapped. She takes a step toward me, reaching out. "Charlie, I'm sorry. I—"

I put my hand up flat to stop her. "Don't." I shake my head as tears begin to trail down my cheeks. "Don't you even dare, Gabby." I shrug and let out a small gasp as I try to tamp down the sobs threatening to break free. "How could you?" Then I turn and flee, not wanting to hear another lie from her lips.

I take a taxi home, strip out of the harlot dress Gabby appropriately dressed me in, and change into a pair of sweats and a t-shirt. I had a good cry in the car, probably making my ride home one of the driver's most interesting of the night. But once I walked through my door, anger took hold and seeped into my pores.

After I changed, I walked around the apartment and picked up every trace of Trey I could find and placed them in a box. Now, I'm sitting at my small dinette table, watching the minutes tick by on the clock while I wait for Trey to ring my buzzer. There are so many thoughts swirling around in my head that I'm dizzy.

All this time, I've been lied to. Trey lied about who he was and what he was really doing all those nights he told me he was working. I shiver when I think of every time I've slept with him without protection in the last seven weeks. How could he do that knowingly? How could he not protect me against that? I scoff out loud. Maybe, in his own demented way, he thought by not telling me, he was protecting me.

I look around my apartment and think about every moment we've spent here. The times we've laid on my couch watching movies with popcorn, eating at this very table, him chasing me around the room before throwing me over his shoulder and carrying me like a caveman to the bedroom to have his way with me. Deliciously happy moments. Every single one of them. I may be naive about some things, but I know none of that was fake. I know he truly cares for me. But when it's all based on a lie, started with a lie that only grew in size, does it really even matter anymore?

Before I can answer my own question, the buzzer sounds, jumpstarting my heart into a frenzied rhythm. I rise and walk to my door, pressing the button to release the lock downstairs, and then release the locks on the door before moving to sit back down at the table. My ass is barely in the chair when he knocks once on the door and bursts through, his expression one of torment.

I'm ashamed to admit that a wave of desire washes over me at the sight of him. He's so unbelievably gorgeous. And in a suit, even more so. It reminds me of the night I met him. The dark grey of the shirt meshes so well with the black silk of the suit he's wearing, making him appear almost regal. And his goddamn lips, so full and red as he licks them, his nerves evident as he moves toward me and kneels in front of me.

He takes my hands in his and rests his head on top of them. "I'm sorry. I'm so, so sorry. I should have told you this and so much more weeks ago."

It dawns on me then that he must have talked to Gabby, because he dives right into an apology without even explaining what for. Maybe she called him? Who knows at this point how deep their little collusion runs? But it's obvious to me when he doesn't even explain what he's sorry for that they've spoken. My heart lurches at the continued deception, and I pull my hands from his, pushing his head up as I do.

"It really doesn't matter anymore, Trey." I try to keep my voice monotone so I don't betray how badly I'm shaking inside. He lifts his head, his eyes searching for mine, but I look away and move to stand, unable to bear him this close to me. I hear him rise behind me and take two steps toward me and then stop when I begin talking again.

"I just really need to know if I should get tested." I spin around, surprised to find he's only inches away from me, so I take a step blindly back. "How could you sleep with me and not use protection?"

He looks up at the ceiling, closing his eyes for a moment, then lowers them again, meeting mine. "You don't need to get tested."

"And I guess I should just believe you?" I retort, wanting to fight. Wanting to expel some of the anger burning inside of me.

He takes a step closer to me. Only one. "Charlotte, I've slept with two women as an employee of the agency. The first was one of the very first assignments I had. I thought it was what I was supposed to do. I didn't realize I could say no. I did it and hated myself for it after. That was almost two years ago and I wore a condom." He pauses and locks eyes with me. "The second was you." He pauses a moment, letting that sink in, and then continues. "But you're the first woman I *ever* had sex with bare."

"Lucky me," I reply, wanting to hurt him in any way that I can. I want him to feel like shit. To feel just a fraction of what I'm feeling right now.

He reaches out and grabs my arm. "Stop acting like you don't care. Like none of this matters."

I wrench free of his hold and glare at him. "It doesn't matter, Trey. Or Maddox. Or whatever I should call you! Not anymore. Because this is over!" He balks and rears back a step as my voice raises to a scream on my last sentence.

"No," he whispers.

The bitterness in my stomach curls up and spews out in a cackled laugh. "No?"

"I'm in love with you." He reaches out to me, but I step back out of his grasp. He says it again like he can't believe I didn't hear it the first time. "I'm in love with you, Charlotte."

The words pierce my heart, and I feel like it's bleeding as warmth spreads across my chest. To have him say these words to me now. Of all times. I huff out a breath and blink back the tears threatening to fall again. "You're in love with me?" I chuff out a laugh in disbelief. "Is this what you call love? Taking money to fuck me and then lying to me about it? Taking money to do who knows what with other women every weekend? Coming to my apartment after? Sleeping with me? Is that what you call love?"

"Charlotte, please." His voice is anguished as he pleads with me. "Working at the agency is just a means to an end. I provide a service. I escort, escort being the key word, not fuck, not screw, not even kiss these women. I'm their company for a dinner, or an event, or sometimes even a funeral. That's it. It means nothing."

I look at him, smiling sadly. "It means something, Trey, or you wouldn't have kept it a secret from me."

His chin drops to his chest as he sighs in defeat. He knows he's lost. But I feel like I've lost more. More than he even realizes. I'm done. I can't fight about this with him anymore. My heart is shattered. My mind exhausted. My body numb.

I walk over to the table and pick up his box of things, then swipe the envelope I have under it and turn to him. "Here."

He stares at the small box of items. It's a pair of scrubs, three t-shirts, a toothbrush, deodorant, and a couple pairs of underwear. I thrust it out to him, and he finally reaches out to take it, a stricken look on his face. I rush past him and open the door. "I want you to go."

He turns and looks at me, his eyes dark, his body tightening in what I know is anger, but then he walks forward to the door. "I'm not giving up. I know I screwed up. But this," he looks up at me, "what we have, it's not a lie."

"What it is, is over." I hand him the envelope and then look at the door. I sweep my hand toward the opening.

"What's this?" He looks at the paper in his hands.

I push him out the door then look him straight in the eye. "It's for your time." And then I slam the door behind him, locking it before sliding down it, my body shaking as I try to hold back the sobs ripping up from my chest.

CHAPTER SEVENTEEN

~Trey~

I shift the box under one arm and tear open the envelope, stopping when I see the money inside. I pull it out and count five one-hundred dollar bills. Her words make perfect sense now, and the pain that stabs me in the chest takes my breath away. I let the box fall to the floor and turn to the door and pound on it. "Charlotte!"

I can hear her crying on the other side, and I growl in frustration when she doesn't open it. I slam my fist against the flat wood and call out to her one more time. "Charlotte, please! Open the door."

I hear her move, and I stand straight, waiting to see if it opens but sag when I hear the patter of her footsteps leading away instead. I pound my fist against the door again, this time in resignation, my head falling against the wood. "I'm sorry," I mutter, knowing it doesn't matter anymore because she's not listening.

After what feels like seconds but is probably more like minutes, I heave myself off the door and bend over to pick up the

box. I stuff the money back in the envelope and shove it under her
door then leave, my fucking insides torn to shreds.

I walk into the hospital Monday morning, knowing that at
least I'll get to see her here, but learn, after not seeing her
signed in and questioning one of the other nurses, that
Charlotte's switched all her shifts for the next two weeks to
midnights. I'm pissed that I'm not going to see her but even
angrier that she feels like she has to turn her life upside down to
avoid me.

I pull my phone out of my pocket and send her a text. Probably
the thirtieth I've sent since Saturday night.

-I would have switched to nights.

And then, because I don't think I can say it enough.

-I'm sorry. And I miss you.

I'm not surprised when she doesn't respond. She hasn't yet,
and I don't expect she will to these texts either. I'm just happy she
hasn't blocked my number. At least I know she is receiving
my words.

"You look like shit." I jerk my head up from my phone, Gabby
leaning over the desk in front of me. "Forget how to use a razor?"

I lift my hand and run my fingers over the stubble on my face.
I know I look like shit. I've hardly slept the last two nights and
barely managed to drag my ass in here this morning. I only did
with the hopes of seeing Charlotte. I shrug then look her in the
eye. "Have you seen her?"

Her gaze drops to the counter where her finger is tracing a
small circle around and around. "No, and she's not answering my
texts or calls either." She looks back up at me, a sad look in her
eyes. "I told her you didn't take the money. That you were only
supposed to woo her, not sleep with her. Just make her feel
special. That you slept with her because you truly liked her and

not as a job." She frowns, her finger stopping its movement. "Well, I left it in one of the thousand messages I sent to her anyway."

"I should have told her." I lay my hand over hers, trying to offer her some comfort. "I should have told her from the very beginning about Temptations. About my job there. It's not your fault, Gabby."

She pushes away from the counter, pulling her hand out from under mine as she stands straight. "We were both wrong, and now we're both just going to have to wait and see if she forgives us."

I nod my head. I know she's right and that I probably do need to give Charlotte time to cool off and then, maybe, she'll hopefully listen to some of what I said. But it's killing me. Not having her to talk to, to laugh with, to share my days with has left a void I wasn't even aware she had filled. Or that needed filling.

I'd already made the decision to quit the agency. My heart hasn't been in it for a long time anyway, and while meeting Charlotte made that even more real, losing her solidified it. I told Trick yesterday and warned him I would probably have to move out to find a cheaper place. Being true to form, he told me to fuck off, that he didn't care if I lived there rent free, and that his grandmother didn't need the damn money anyway.

He was pissed, however, that I'm leaving the agency, which struck me as odd because we never work together. The only thing we have in common at the agency is Cory. He has a completely different set of clientele, given the fact he's more than willing to stick his dick in anything that throws money at him. He doesn't even need the money. His parents would give him anything he needed if he asked.

But I know he isn't working at Temptations for the money. He does it as an escape. A way to avoid the reality he's trying so hard to keep buried in pain and sex. I also know it's going to catch up to him sooner or later, but somehow, he's managed to stay ahead of his demons.

I pull myself from my thoughts and turn my attention back to Gabby. "You still spending time with Trick?"

She shakes her head and gives me a weird smile. "Kind of."

I cock my head, curiosity piquing my interest. "Kind of? What's that mean?"

She looks around to make sure no one is in listening distance and then leans closer to me, her voice low. "He's been helping me to decide if maybe I want to go to work at the Agency."

My head snaps back in surprise as my mouth falls open. "What? Why? Aren't you like Little Miss Richy Rich?" I don't mean for the question to be rude but know it probably comes across like that.

"Because I like men." She looks at me like I'm a dummy. "And why the hell not?" She drums her fingers across the top of the desk. "It's not like I'm looking to get serious with anyone. I like meeting new people. I like having fun. Why not get paid for it?"

"You know it's illegal to get paid for the sex part, right?" I reply, wanting to make sure that Trick has really explained how things work.

"I'm not doing it for the money, asshole, but yeah." She snorts back at me. "I couldn't give two shits about the money. If I like a guy, it's my prerogative what I chose to do, right?"

I raise my brows and lift my shoulders. "I guess it is." I've never met two more opposite people than Gabby and Charlotte and can't help but wonder how they even became friends.

"But listen." She looks up at me, her eyes serious. "Don't say anything to Charlie. Okay? She wouldn't understand."

I nod and scoff. "That shouldn't be a problem since she's not talking to me anyway." I tap my knuckles on the counter and then turn to walk away. "Okay, I guess I better go fix some sick people. I'll talk to you later."

"Later, asshole," she calls after me, never disappointing me with her true colors.

~Charlotte~

I t's been ten days since I slammed the door behind Trey and my heart shattered into millions of pieces. I didn't realize it until the next day, after every molecule in my body ached from missing him, but I had fallen in love with him, too. Even after knowing what I learned, it didn't lessen what my heart wanted. And make no doubt about it, my heart wanted him.

But my head, it wasn't going there. I should have followed the advice I set out for myself back at the beginning of the summer and stuck with B.O.B. I certainly wouldn't be in the mess I'm in now. I look down at the three sticks laying on my bathroom counter and let out a shaky laugh. Just my damn luck. All three are positive. I'm fucking pregnant. With my gigolo's baby.

I laugh, because if I don't, I'll fall spectacularly apart. What makes it worse; I don't even have Gabby to share this with. To help me freak out about it in only the way that Gabby could have, knowing she would have made me feel better afterwards. At least I know now that I wasn't feeling nauseous because of what happened with Trey. I laugh out loud then, realizing, actually, it's all Trey's damn fault.

I pick up the sticks and shove them deep into the drawer of the vanity so I don't have to look at them anymore. I'm going to have to make some decisions, but I'm not ready for that yet. I can't be that far along. My period is only a couple weeks late, and I've only been sleeping with Trey for about seven weeks. Stupid damn birth control that didn't work. Stupid bare back sex I had with Trey and his damn perfect cock.

I need to get ready for work, so I strip out of my pajamas and step into the shower. When I lather the soap over my body, I lay my hands over my still flat belly, fully realizing that there's a life growing inside of me now. A life I created with Trey. I wonder what he would think if he knew that, right now, right this very second, a part of him is growing inside of me. My heart clenches in pain as I realize I'm going to have to tell him. It's the right thing to do. I just wish my heart would stop arguing with my head.

An hour later, I walk into the hospital, surprised when I see Gabby sitting behind the nurse's station. She should have left two hours ago. Her shift ends at five, mine starts at seven. I breeze by her, holding my nose in the air, and go to the locker room to change. Maybe she's just finishing up some late charts. But no, when I walk back out to the station, she's still sitting there. I come up beside her and pull the summary sheet off the counter so I can see what's going on in the department.

"Hey." She looks over at me. "How ya doing?"

"Why are you here?" I reply, my tone curt.

"I'm good, thanks," she states sarcastically. "Pam called out. I'm covering 'til eleven. Janet will be in then to take the rest of the shift." She rises from the chair. "I'll try to stay out of your way the next four hours." And she walks away.

My pulse, which was racing like a wildfire, starts to slow down a minute after she leaves. I hate fighting with her. I know what she did, at least the original part she played in setting up Trey and me, wasn't meant to be harmful. But that's not what I'm mad at her for. It's that she knew what Trey did and kept that a secret from me. I don't understand why she would keep that hidden from me when she knew it was something that would be a big deal to me.

I pick up two charts for patients waiting to be seen by one of the E.R. docs when she appears beside me and pushes me back down in my chair, an 'ompf' sounding from me as I land in it. I stare up in shock at her.

"Okay, enough." She drops her body into the chair next to mine. "Let's have this out because I'm sick to death of not being able to talk to you, and I miss you. So, go, give it to me."

I look at her then roll my eyes heavily. "It always has to come back to you and how you're feeling."

This time, it's her who rolls her eyes. "Stop being so fucking dramatic about everything, Charlie." She scoots her chair closer to mine. "So I didn't tell you Trey's little secret. Big fucking deal. For once, I decided to mind my own business. And you know why?"

I squint my eyes and grind my teeth. "Oh, I'm dying to know why, Gabs, why you thought it was better to keep me in the dark that my boyfriend is a goddamn gigolo!"

"Oh, for fuck's sake, Charlie! He's not a damn gigolo, so just stop it!" She grabs my chair by the arms and shakes it, jostling me around. "You were happy. So damn happy. I've never seen you like that. I didn't want to ruin that. And because Trick told me that Trey never sleeps with his clients. Ever. So, I trusted what he felt for you was real."

"You don't think it would have been good for me to know he was working as an escort? I mean, come on, Gabby, really?"

"No, not when I saw the way he looked at you." She shrugs. "I'm sorry. I wasn't trying to hurt you. Really. I just wanted you to be happy for once."

"By lying to me?" I snap back.

"Only by omission," she tries as a defense. "Besides, he quit."

"What?" I sit up straight, thinking she's referring to his job here at the hospital. "When?"

She blinks. "I think the day after you found out about it."

"Wait, are we talking about the same thing? He's not here anymore?"

She rolls her eyes again. "Keep up, Charlie. No. He quit working at Temptations."

I'm quiet for a minute as that sinks in. He's sent me at least fifty texts since we broke up, but I haven't read a single one. I can't. I'm afraid I'll give in to my heart, and I want to be smart this time. Besides, it doesn't change the fact that he did work there when we were together and kept it a secret.

"He's a fucking mess, Charlie." Her voice is laced with concern as she relays this information. "He's been like a zombie around here, and he's practically sporting a full beard. Do you think you can maybe throw him a bone?"

"Gabby, it's so much more complicated than me just forgiving him."

"Is it though? Really?" Her hand moves over mine and pulls it into her own. "It's obvious you're both in love with each other. Are you sure you want to throw that away because he acted like a guy and made a stupid decision? You know that they tend to do that, right? A lot."

"He was with other women every weekend, Gabby." I look down and swing my head back and forth. "Instead of with me."

"It was just a job to him, Charlie." She squeezes my hand. "He provided them with his company. That's it. Try and equate it to him helping people when they come through the doors here. It's a service. He probably puts his hands on more people here than he ever did on one of those dates." She chuckles.

"It's a little different than that, Gabs, and you know it."

She nods her head. "I know. I do. But, Charlie, he does love you. Of that I'm sure." She lets go of my hand and sits up straight. "Are you sure you want to throw that away?"

I look up at her, my lips curved downward. "I'm not sure of anything anymore."

"Well, can we be friends again, even if you aren't sure about him yet?" She looks at me hopefully.

"Gabby, you know I love you. I do." I rise from my chair and stand above her. "But if you ever *omit* something like this to me again…"

She stands then and throws her arms around me in a hug. "I promise. Never again."

We both pull apart and smile at each other, relief on both our faces. I'm about to tell her my really big problem when the front door swishes open and Trey walks in carrying a woman in his arms. "Can I get some help here?"

CHAPTER EIGHTEEN

~Trey~

M y arms are trembling from exertion when I finally lower Karen onto a gurney Gabby brought out to me. My heart stutters in my chest when my eyes capture Charlotte's, the first time I've laid eyes on her in almost two weeks, but I need to concentrate on the moment at hand, so I stuff my feelings away for now.

We maneuver the bed back into one of the exam rooms, and I give a rundown of what occurred. "This is Karen Perry, eighty-two years old. We were eating dinner and she collapsed. I'm not sure if she's on any medications. Pulse is really weak, breathing shallow."

I point to Charlotte. "Start an I.V. and let's get some blood drawn so we can see what's going on." Then I point to Gabby. "We need an E.K.G., now. Let's see what's going on with her heart."

The girls both move to begin their assigned tasks. I reach out to Charlotte and graze my fingers against her neck, her body tensing when she feels me, her head turning, her eyes landing on mine. "Can I use this?"

She looks down and realizes I'm reaching for her stethoscope and then nods, lowering her head as I lift it off her neck. We all work in silence, the tension thick in the room, Karen finally waking up when some fluids start flowing into her system. She's groggy at first but aware, and relief surges through me.

"Dinner with me not exciting enough for you anymore?" I tease as I sit next to her. "I could have just brought you here if you wanted to see where I work."

"I'm sorry, dear." She reaches for my hand with her fingers and pulls it into hers. "That was a bit scary."

I nod in agreement. "Can you tell me what you felt like before you passed out?"

She talks to me for a few minutes about her symptoms but then stops when Charlotte sweeps into the room and moves to adjust some of the settings on the I.V.

"Is this her?" She's trying to say it discreetly, but it's impossible in a room this size, and Charlotte smiles down at her in response.

"I'm Charlie." Charlotte lays her petite hand over Karen's and holds it gently. "Trey's told me an awful lot about you. Almost had me a little jealous." She giggles and smiles warmly down at her.

"Oh, but he loves you so." I see Karen squeeze and hold onto Charlotte's hand as she continues to talk. "I don't think you've got anything to worry about there." I feel heat traveling up my neck as she turns and looks over at me and then back to Charlotte. "His heart belongs only to you. That's something to treasure, dear." She gives her hand a final squeeze, releasing it with a tender pat, and then swings her gaze over to me. "I think I'm going to take a little nap, Trey. I'm feeling a bit tired."

I'm sure it's some of the medicine we've got pumping into her, but I'm anxious to get the blood work results to confirm it. All her symptoms point to a heart attack, and I want to see if I can get a clearer picture of how extensive it might have been. I smile down at her then place a kiss on her forehead. "Okay, sweet dreams."

I look up to find Charlotte watching me, a strange expression on her face. She turns away when she notices me looking at her and moves to exit the room. "Charlotte?"

She stops, a heavy breath rising from her chest before she faces me again. "Yes."

"It's nice to see you." I want to punch myself in the face for saying such a lame thing, but I don't want her to leave the room.

She nods. "I'm going to go see if we can get Mrs. Perry a room up in the I.C.U." Then she scurries out of the room like a mouse being chased.

An hour later, we've confirmed Karen's had a pretty serious heart attack. She's transferred to the I.C.U. where they can observe her and run further tests on how extensive, and put together a plan for her recovery. I stay with her for another hour and then slip away when she finally seems to be sleeping peacefully.

It's almost one in the morning, and I have to be here in six hours, so I head back down to the E.R. to see if I can find an empty bed to sleep in for a few hours. It's quiet when I walk on the floor, only two rooms occupied, and those patients seem to be resting comfortably. Out of habit, I read each of the charts and note that they've been seen and treated and are now just waiting to be discharged. That process can be a little slower in the middle of the night, especially if we don't have people lined up at the doors waiting to be seen.

I'm stalling. I know I am. I know Charlotte's around the corner, and I need to ask her which room I can crash in. I'm afraid of how she's going to look at me. I don't want to see any pain or confusion in her eyes when she looks at me, but I know she has every right to those feelings. I've wished about a thousand times in the last week that I could turn back the clock and change some of the decisions I made regarding the secrets I kept from her. I tried to tell myself it didn't matter. That what I was doing wasn't hurting anyone. But I was wrong. I hurt her, and I don't know if she's going to be able to forgive me for that.

I lean against the wall and let my head fall back against it, my eyes closing in exhaustion as I continue to roll all these thoughts around in my brain.

"Oh!" My eyes shoot open and I push myself away from the wall when I hear her voice. "Trey. What are you doing?" She's standing beside me, holding a stack of sheets and blankets.

"Honestly?" I respond flatly.

"Well, that would be a nice change of pace," she quips.

I cock my head. I guess I deserve that. "I was procrastinating."

Her brows rise as she waits for me to continue.

"I'm back on in a few hours. I just want to know if there's a room I can crash in 'til then. Doesn't make sense to go home and come back again."

"And you were procrastinating, why?" She tilts her head in question.

I look down and cross my arms over my chest, nerves kicking into high gear. "I, uh, don't want to get in your way. You know, I'm trying to be respectful of your space."

She looks at me for a second, her teeth gnawing on her bottom lip, causing a new wave of feelings to wash over me at the memories it sparks. "I'm a big girl, Trey." She walks past me. "Come on. I was just going to make up some beds. I'll show you which one you can use."

I turn to follow after her and pick up my pace so I'm walking beside her and then reach over to take the linens from her. She pulls them to her chest and gives me a hard look. "I've got them."

"I just wanted to help," I try to explain.

"I'm fine." Ugh. Two of the worst words to come from a woman's mouth. I don't know a lot of things, but I do know that when a woman tells you she's fine, she most definitely is not. I shut my mouth and just continue to follow her down the hallway until she turns and kicks a door open with her foot. She walks into the room and plops the pile she's holding down on the counter.

I stand there, so she leans over, brushing her body against mine, and flips the switch on the wall to turn the light on. "You can sleep here."

She pulls a sheet off the pile and throws her arms out in front of her, the sheet opening in a wide arc as it floats down over the bed. She moves to one side of the mattress and begins tucking in the edges to secure it. I hustle to the opposite side and copy what she's doing, an operation I perfected while I was in the Army.

She leans over to smooth the sheet at the same time I do, and our foreheads collide. "Ouch!" She rears back, her hand coming up to hold her head.

"Oh my God! Sorry!" I move quickly around the bed and slide her hand off her forehead so I can investigate. I run my thumb over a small raised bump, already a little red. I'm about to declare that she'll live when my eyes roam lower, locking onto hers. She's staring up at me, her brows slightly furrowed, her bottom lip starting to quiver as I stare back at her.

I blink when I see drops begin spill over the edge of her lids and track slowly down her cheeks. Without thinking, I lean forward and begin peppering kisses along the trails, trying to capture anymore before they can fall. "Don't cry, baby," I whisper between kisses, which only seems to make her cry harder. "Please don't cry." My kisses start to linger each time I drop my lips onto her cheek until she tilts her head up and slides her mouth over mine, her arms moving to wrap around my neck as she clings onto me.

I slide my arms around, pulling her to me, enveloping her in my embrace, my lips continuing to caress hers as I feel the small splatters of her tears hitting her cheeks. Her tongue swipes against my lips, coaxing them to open, then laps against mine as her arms tighten around me. A second later, she tears her lips away, her cheek sliding up against mine as she presses her entire body into me and begins sobbing.

I'm momentarily stunned but then sit back on the bed, pulling

161

her into my lap, cradling her like a child as she rocks against me. I hold her against me, pressing kisses to her locks, slightly damp now from sweat, until her tears finally begin to subside. Her hand lays flat on my chest and pushes against me as she pulls back to look up at me.

"I'm so mad at you." She clenches her mouth together and lets out a little growl then looks back up at me. "But I also miss you so much."

I know it's not much, but it's a start. She's letting me hold her. She's letting me comfort her. Starting to let me back in again. I know they're baby steps, but they give me hope that maybe she'll actually forgive me.

~Charlotte~

I'm not really sure what caused me to finally break. If it was three positive pregnancy tests I took earlier that day, or Gabby and I making up, or Karen Perry telling me that Trey's heart belongs only to me. Something started to thaw the ice I built up around my heart in the last ten days, and I started to feel again. Part of that was letting go of all the hurt and anger I had bottled up inside myself over those days since finding out about Trey.

I let him hold me for much longer than I should have. I know Janet, the other nurse on duty with me tonight, is covering the front, and unless we get a rush of people, probably won't even notice I'm missing, but I still feel guilty that I'm still sitting here on his lap.

"I should probably get back to work." I push myself up and try to slide out of his lap, but he tightens his hold on me. I turn my head to look up at him. "And you should probably get some sleep before your shift tomorrow morning."

"There are probably a lot of things I should do. Or should have done." He speaks softly, his beard scratching against the tresses of my hair. "But all I really want to do right now is keep holding you." He lets out a breath, it's heat trickling down over my head. "I've missed you, Charlotte. So much. My body literally aches for you."

I bop my head under his chin, understanding exactly how he feels. Because I felt it, too. Every single time I laid in my bed and closed my eyes, every touch, every kiss, every moment we spent together seemed to play like a revolving record in my mind.

"I'm not working at the agency anymore. I just want you to know that I quit."

"I know," I mumble against his chest.

"You know?"

"Gabby told me." I let out a sigh, my brain starting to kick into gear, overriding my heart. "It still doesn't change what happened. You kept this secret from me. You were spending your time with other women when you could have been with me."

He doesn't say anything for a few minutes then finally speaks. "I wish I could give you a reason or an excuse that would make what I did not so big. But when I factor it against what I risked by hiding what I did from you, no excuse is enough." I feel his shoulders lift and then lower. "I was stupid. I thought my reasons for working at Temptations justified my behavior. I know now that it didn't. It just hurt you and made me realize how weak I really am. Knowing I lost you in the end made me realize just how bad the decisions I made were."

I listen to what he says and then nod my head, not sure how to respond. He shifts me then, adjusting me so that he's looking down into my eyes. "I am sorry though, Charlotte. So sorry I hurt you. Sorry I wasn't smart enough to know right away that you are worth so much more than how I made you feel. But I meant it when I told you I loved you." He pauses, a breath leaving him. "I love you."

"I believe you, Trey." I say softly. "I do." I close my eyes for a minute and then look back at him. "I'm just trying to figure out a way to let go of all the hurt, all the jealousy I feel knowing you were with these other women. Because I realized something, too, when this happened." I swallow and lift my eyes to his, my voice trembling. "I fell in love with you, too. And not being with you hurts more than all the other hurts combined."

I'm surprised when Trey starts blinking rapidly but fails at his attempt to hold back tears, as they still escape around his lashes. "Does that mean you forgive me?"

I nod my head. "It means I want to try."

His eyes crinkle as a wide grin lifts his cheeks, and then he pulls me to him, his lips seeking and finding mine, sealing the promises we just made to each other.

$\approx$

It's been almost two weeks since that night in the hospital when I confessed my feelings to Trey and told him I would try. Things have been amazing. Letting go of the anger and the hurt caused by his lie was easier than I thought it would be. I think because I knew without doubt that he loved me. I believe his lies weren't to hurt me. Plus, I learned that it takes so much more energy to hold onto all the anger, instead of letting it go and learning to forgive. Especially when I have so much at stake.

I place my hand on my stomach and realize I still have my own secret to tell. I haven't told him yet, and I know I need to. At first, I waited until I knew if Trey and I could really move past what had happened between us. It's more than clear to me that we have and that we're moving forward.

I finished my last night shift two days ago and am switching back to days starting Monday. It's Friday, and Trey finished up his shift at seven and is on his way here. We both have this weekend off, so I know it's time to tell him. I just pray it doesn't send him running. God knows I'm terrified of this thing growing inside of me; what it means and how it's going to change my entire world. I have no idea what Trey thinks of children, let alone if he wants any. Our relationship is barely three months old. Sometimes, even if you love someone, something like this is just too much.

The door buzzer yanks me out of my deep thoughts, a smile breaking across my face, knowing it's him. I release the lock and then swing my door open as I wait for him to emerge at the top of the steps. When he does and sees me, his face lights up as he takes long strides down the hallway, scooping me up with one arm when he reaches me.

"God, I missed you, today!" His lips brush against my hair as he speaks but move quickly to my mouth as he lowers me back to the floor, backing me up into my apartment, slamming my door behind him with a kick of his foot. The backpack he's holding in his other hand clunks to the floor, and then that hand wraps firmly around my waist. I kick my legs up and wrap them around his waist, noticing he's already hard as my core presses against him as he heads toward my bedroom.

I tear my mouth from his. "I see you came prepared." I giggle and loosen my arms from his neck so I can lean back to look into his eyes.

"I think that's the Boy Scout's creed, but it works." His mouth cocks up on one side in a naughty grin. He lays me back on the bed and then takes a step back. I'm wearing one of his t-shirts and nothing else and know he notices when his eyes fall at the juncture between my legs and his brows lift in approval.

"I see I'm not the only one that's prepared." He slides the stethoscope still sitting around his neck off then walks over to my bedside table and sets it down. Keeping his eyes locked on mine, he reaches behind his neck and pulls his scrub shirt off next.

I never get tired of that view, the rippled expanse of muscle and silky skin that I get to claim as mine. I wiggle my fingers out, making it clear I want him closer.

He chuckles and then leans over me, snatching the stethoscope off the table as he does, slipping it around his neck. "Let's see if your heart can handle what I'm about to do to you." His tongue darts out, wetting his lips as his fingers grasp the hem of the t-shirt and drag it slowly up my torso until my breasts are exposed. His hand moves to cup one, my nipple falling between two of his fingers as he presses them tightly together, my back arching off the bed at the exquisite pain.

He flattens his hand then and runs it over both my breasts. "I think I've been feeding you too much. Your breasts are getting bigger." His eyes swing up and latch onto mine. "Not that I'm complaining, mind you."

My heart lurches in my chest and I snag my lip into my teeth, knowing the real reason my breasts are changing, but I don't have a chance to say anything as he drops his mouth to mine and then uses his own teeth to pull my lip out. "You know that drives me fucking crazy," he growls.

"Sorry," I whimper, wet heat pulsing between my legs in arousal.

He shifts back and adjusts the stethoscope so he has an end in each ear and then places the flat disk right next to my left nipple. It peaks from the cold metal so close, and I let out a small gasp as he reaches down and sucks it into his mouth. He releases it a second later, lifting the disk off, a sexy smile planted on his face. "Miss, your heart seems to be beating a little erratically."

I blink my lashes and purse my lips, arching my back slightly off the bed. "Do you have anything to help that, doctor?" I'm completely up for this little game he's playing.

He chuckles and stands back beside the bed, pulling the scope off his head, placing it back on the table. His gaze shifts down, and he pulls the drawer of the table open, his brows rising in reaction to his eyes growing wide. He turns to look at me as he pulls something out and holds it up to me, my face heating.

"Well, look what we have here. This might fix your problem." He turns my long, hard dildo in his hand then smiles when he realizes he simply has to twist the bottom to turn it on, which he does, a vibrating sound radiating through the air softly. "Uh-huh," he hums appreciatively and then moves to kneel between my legs.

"I can explain," I joke, because he's heard Gabby and I refer to B.O.B. more than once, and we finally had to explain to him that 'it' was my other boyfriend.

He cocks an eyebrow as he takes the flesh colored tool and drags it in a slow circle around my nipple. "I don't think that's necessary." And then he leans over and licks the hard point before sucking it into his mouth, trailing the vibrator down my center until it's between my legs. I flinch and my legs move to close when he brushes it against my clit, the intensity of it even more sensitive with the new hormones that have invaded my body.

"Oooh," he coos as he lets go of my nipple and moves lower to hover over my core. "This is going to be fun." He places a hand on one of my legs and pushes it out, pressing the vibrator hard as he sweeps it up and down my pussy, spreading my wetness over me. He teases me, barely grazing my clit but never applying pressure, my hips arching toward him every time. I moan in frustration, wanting more, eliciting another sexy chuckle from him.

His scrub bottoms are still on, but I can see the outline of his cock through the thin material, and I reach for the crown, squeezing my hand around it when I find it. His hips fly forward, and a low grumble of pleasure rolls up from his chest. "Sweet Jesus, yes." He uses one hand to untie the laces holding up his pants, and I push the material down, slipping my hand over the hot skin of his cock, gripping it tightly.

He moves his hips to help me slide my hand more easily up and down and then shifts his focus back to me, a sinister smile on his face as I feel him shift the vibrator and begin to slowly slide it up my channel. I clench my eyes, trying to press back the orgasm I already feel beckoning, and shake my head back and forth against the pillow. "Oh, God…" I drawl out in a long breath as he pushes it all the way in then turns up the vibration to full power. He draws it in and out several times, and when he senses I'm close, angles the toy so it smashes up against my clit, and I scream his name as my pussy explodes. A million shards of light spread across my dark lids as my core throbs around the vibrator. He leaves it in for only a second then shifts over me as he slides it out and replaces it in one hard shove with his own cock.

I can barely move as he surges his hips hard against mine, pushing himself past my still convulsing pussy, my mouth open wide in pure bliss. He pumps into me ferociously, his balls slapping against my ass every time he slams into me, his hands gripping onto my arms hauling me up against his chest as I feel him come. He cries out my name, his fingers digging deeply into the muscles of my back as he continues to pump into me, the throbbing in my pussy seeming to draw out his release.

His hips finally come to a rest, his hot breaths panting over the top of my head, his grip on me relaxing only slightly. "I love you, Charlotte," he says between gasps, his lips sliding to my ear as he whispers the words and then to my lips as he kisses me savagely, my pussy throbbing around him again as he does.

When he pulls away, he rests he forehead against mine and I look into his eyes. "I love you, too."

He drops a soft kiss to my lips and then slowly shifts and extricates himself from me, a slow lazy river of cum dripping from me as he pulls free. Like always, he motions for me to stay, and he walks out of the room. I know he's going to get something to clean me up.

I fall back in the bed and let out a long, dreamy sigh. I'm in love. With Trey Riley.

CHAPTER NINETEEN

~Trey~

I blink my eyes, trying to focus in the morning light of the room, and smile when I look down and feel Charlotte curled up against me like a kitten. I want every morning to be like this. I blink again, absorbing my own thought, and then shake off the immediate fear I felt. I'm in love with her. I can't imagine being with anyone else. Waking up to her in my arms, I realize I want this every damn day. When I'm not with her, I just ache until she's with me again.

I reach down and stroke my fingers over her cheek, sweeping back the hair that's covering her gorgeous face, and smile when I see her eyes start to open. "Good morning, baby," I say softly.

"Morning," she mumbles back and scoots her body deeper into mine. She's always slower to wake up in the mornings than me.

I take a breath and hold it, knowing what I'm about to do is probably a little crazy, but I exhale and do it anyway. "Let's move in together."

Her eyes pop open, followed by her body as it sits up next to me. "What?" Shock is splayed across her face, and I can clearly see she's not entirely sure she heard me correctly, so I repeat it.

"Let's move in together." I gather her taut form in my hands and guide her to lay back against my chest. "I like waking up with you every morning and sleeping with you every night." I chuckle lightly at the double-meaning around the last part of my last sentence. "I want to be able to do this every day."

I can feel her heart beating in a fast staccato over my chest as she considers what I've said, and making me nervous, I keep talking, trying to convince her. "I mean, I know it's probably too soon. But, if I'm honest with you, I just don't see a place in my life anymore unless you're in it beside me."

She still hasn't answered, so I shift under her and lift her eyes to mine. I'm surprised when I see tears glistening in her eyes. "What's wrong?" I say in shock.

She shifts so she's sitting up and then nods her head. "I love you, Trey. You know that, right?"

My brows furrow and I nod. "I do. I know you do." I cup her cheek and lean forward to brush some of the tears away. "I love you, too."

She nods against my hand and then moves to slide out of the bed. She stands before me a minute, and it's hard not to notice how unbelievably gorgeous she is, even rumpled from sleep. My cock starts to stir awake. "I'll be right back."

I sit up straighter, more worried now, and run my fingers through my hair. She's back in just a minute and is holding something in her hand.

"I want to move in with you. I truly do. More than anything." She pauses then and looks down at whatever's hidden in her hand. "But, I think we might need a bigger place."

I tilt my head in confusion as she climbs back on the bed and gives me what she had in her hand. I take it, and as soon as it's between my fingers, the light bulb clicks and my entire world tilts.

I swear, I think I actually feel a shift in the universe as my heart stutters in my chest and I look at the bold lettering on the stick in my hand: POSITIVE. "You're pregnant?"

She nods, her teeth gnawing her bottom lip into a tender pulp, her hands wringing together in her lap. "Uh-huh."

I look at the stick and then back at her again, my eyes falling on her stomach this time then moving up to her breasts. Her softer, more tender breasts. My brain clicks again. I move my eyes back up to her face and smile. "You're pregnant."

She nods again, a tentative smile starting to curve her mouth up. "Only a little bit right now."

I know I should be freaking out. My girlfriend, that I just barely got back together with, is knocked up. But I'm not. I'm almost thirty years old, and I know I'm completely and utterly in love with this girl sitting in front of me, so I'm not. The order with which we've done things in has been completely fucked up, but I don't for an instant think any of it's wrong.

I move to sit up on my knees and snake my hands out to rest on her flat stomach and then look into her eyes that are still shining with small tears. "There's a baby in here?" I'm still in shock but trying to absorb this life altering news.

She shakes her head up and down. "Our baby, Trey," she whispers, her hands falling in my hair as I lean forward and start pressing kisses against her belly.

I pull back and slide my arms around her body to haul her up against me. "We're having a baby."

Her chest vibrates as she giggles against me, her arms sliding around my waist as she snuggles into me. "You're not mad?"

I look down at her in surprise. "Why would I be mad?"

"It's not exactly something we planned," she states, her breath warm against my chest as she speaks. "And I'd understand if it wasn't something you wanted. We've never even talked about this. I certainly didn't mean for this to happen."

She's starting to ramble in worry, so I grip her lightly and push her back so I can look down at her. "*We* did this. Us. Not you." I sweep a kiss against her forehead. "And I know we haven't ever talked about it, but having kids is something I always had in the cards." I chuckle. "Maybe not this soon." I look down at her again. "But, baby, I honestly can't imagine doing this with anyone but you." I watch as relief washes over her features, and I kiss her again. "We'll figure it out. We've got time."

~

And we do figure it out. Three months later, she's standing in the doorway of our new apartment as she barks orders to Trick and me about where to put the couch. "No, not there, guys! Shift it over a couple feet to the left."

Trick's ready to lose his shit but does as he's told, grumbling the entire time. I plop my end of the couch down and then stroll over to her, smiling at the tiny little bump that's just starting to sprout under her t-shirt. She's got that thin Patriots t-shirt on that I love so much, except she's been forced to wear a bra now that her boobs have swollen up a size. It doesn't quench my desire for her one bit though, and I yank her into my arms and kiss her hard.

"If you guys are going to do that, I'm outta here." Trick groans behind us.

I reluctantly release my hold on Charlotte then spin around, punching him lightly in the shoulder. "Shut the fuck up. You're not going anywhere 'til we're done."

"Then get off your bitch and let's go," he chides.

"Hey, that's the mother of my future child." I shove him playfully. "Careful what you call her."

Charlotte strolls over, sliding her arm around my waist as she looks over at Trick. "You know you're going to be over here all the time once she's here, so quit it with the tough guy act."

He looks back and forth between us as a wide grin breaks across his face, his gaze sweeping to look at Charlotte's belly. "Wait, it's a girl?"

We nod frantically, both beaming as we finally get to share the news with someone. "We found out yesterday, brother!"

He walks over and wraps his arms around both of us in a quick hug and then steps back. "Well, I'll be damned. You're having a girl."

I laugh when Charlotte points a finger at him and laughs. "And since you're right upstairs, you know who I'm calling when I need a babysitter!"

Yeah, we moved into the same building I lived in with Trick. We're one floor down, in a nice two-bedroom apartment. Trick pulled some strings with his grandmother, who I've learned is actually good friends with Karen, and managed to talk her into renting us this place at a steal. It's still steep, but on both our salaries, we'll be okay.

And, I sucked up my pride and took Karen up on her offer to let her take care of my school loans. I only agreed to do it on two conditions, one of them hers. One, was that she let me pay her back, with interest, in a monthly payment plan. She finally agreed to that condition but would not, under any conditions, let me tack on the interest. The second, was that we let her be an honorary grandmother to our child. Neither of us have mothers we're able to share that role with, and since Karen doesn't have any children of her own, it was an easy condition to agree to.

We work the rest of the afternoon moving my things up one flight of stairs and unpacking the truck we rented to move Charlotte's things from her old apartment. We've not done much except unpack enough to make up the new king size bed we bought and find towels so we can both take a shower.

I've just paid the delivery guy for our Chinese and place the food on the breakfast bar in front of stools so we can eat. "Come on, baby, stop unpacking for the night and let's eat."

She spins around from the box she's rummaging around in and comes to sit next to me. "Did you get the spring rolls?" She starts pawing over the boxes looking for them.

I chuckle, loving the strange cravings she has and also accommodating them as her belly starts to grow. "They're right here."

We eat, excited to have our first meal in our new apartment, and then clean up. I'm beat and tell her I'm going to head to bed.

"Okay, I'll be in shortly. I'm just gonna finish that one box."

"Okay." It's perfect because I need five minutes to set up in the bedroom. I stroll casually away toward the room, my insides in knots. When she comes in fifteen minutes later, she's pulling her bra out from under her t-shirt, groaning in relief.

"I didn't realize how much I hated those things until I was forced to wear one all the time!" She rubs her hands over her nipples that are now protruding through the fabric, and I have to physically reach down and push my dick into submission, knowing I've got something else planned right now. I watch as she slides her shorts off and then climbs up onto the bed. She bounces a minute and smiles. "This is a big bed." She lifts her brows suggestively. "We can get into all kinds of trouble in this."

I chuckle. "I think I already got you in enough trouble." Then I reach out and caress her belly lovingly. We're having a baby girl. I smile as a warm heat expands my heart.

"Oh, honey, you kept it!" She smiles and looks at the stuffed snow leopard I have sitting up between our pillows. It's kind of squished and a little matted because I used it as a life line for the almost two-weeks we were separated several months ago.

"Of course I did." I give her a warm smile. "It reminds me of you. I told you."

She shuffles closer to me and rubs her hand over my bicep. "You know, I think that's where we actually made this little critter." She looks down and places a hand on the little bump under her shirt.

My brows arch up in surprise, this revelation only adding to what I'm going to do next. "You think?"

She nods again then reaches for the leopard, my heart jolting in anticipation. "I do. Based on the due date, it makes sense." She pulls the stuffed animal to her lap and hugs it against her. "Our own little cub." She frowns and pulls the animal away, looking down at it curiously. "There's something scratchy on here."

I shift off the bed quietly then and move around to her side, dropping to one knee as she investigates what's around the neck of the leopard. I know she's found it when a small gasp sounds from her. "Trey!" Her eyes swing and lock onto mine, the ring between her fingers, the little ribbon I tied it with dangling from the center.

I had a whole speech ready about how much I love her, and about how much I already love our baby, and how I can't imagine living a single day of my life without her. How I hope I live to be a hundred, knowing I'll love her every moment of that time, and promise that it won't matter anyway, because no matter how long I live, I'll love her after anyway, for eternity. But all I can manage in my complete and utter awe of her is, "Will you marry me?"

And it's enough. It's enough for her because she already knows all the things I feel for her and all the dreams I have for us. It's so apparent when she throws her arms around me and replies, "Yes! A thousand times yes." She kisses me then, her whole heart behind it, and then she nods again, her lips breaking from mine. "I'll marry you, Trey."

And they lived happily ever after....

Want more?
Tempting Tricks, Book Two in the Tempting Nights Romance Series will be available early November 2018. You'll get to see more of Trey and Charlotte and learn Trick's story.

There's a little teaser of what you can expect in just a few more pages...

ACKNOWLEDGMENTS

The biggest thank you always goes to my husband and two sons. I'm so lucky to be surrounded by these three amazing men. They are truly the loves of my life, and offer me so much love, support and, most especially, understanding. They understand when I'm head down in my writing and even though they are out of clean underwear, need help with homework, or just some food in the pantry, they continue to love me anyway. I would be a hollow shell without them, and count my blessings every single day for their love.

I have to give credit to my friend Robin for being the inspiration behind the story for Tempting Secrets. I get ideas popping into my head all the time for stories, but when we sat at lunch one day and she giggled behind her hand as she showed me this site she stumbled upon online. (Yeah-I'm not sure what she was looking for to begin with, but who am I to judge ;) lol) The site was for male escorts. Really good looking male escorts. All over the United States, in all the major cities. That's all it took. A story was born and I ran with it. So, thanks Robin for your 'accidental' find.

This was supposed to be a single story when I started writing.

An escort falls in love with one of his clients, and she doesn't even know he's an escort. You know what happens after that... BUT, then, when I was in Reno at the RT Convention, I happened to be hanging out with author Lisa Lang Blakeney and promoter Lauren Valderrama, just talking shop. I was really struggling with how much more I wanted to put into this book and how I could make that happen and learned Lisa was having the same problem with a book she was writing. Lauren told Lisa, 'Just make it a series', like it was the most obvious solution in the world. And so, I took her advice, (okay, I stole her advice to Lisa), and five more book outlines were born. So, if you really liked this book, thank Lauren for the next five...

Thanks to my brother-in-law George, who I affectionately call Jo-Jo, and is a real-life Physician's Assistant for answering all my questions about school requirements and other medically related questions. And to my book bestie and sometimes co-author Haylee Thorne, who is also a registered nurse and read the book to make sure I did all nurses justice. She listens to so many of my ideas when I'm writing, as well as lots of venting when I'm frustrated and I couldn't ask for a better sounding board and friend. Haylee-I flove your face so much it's not even funny. Most of the medical knowledge I have is based on episodes of Greys Anatomy and E.R., so if I was off base anywhere, please accept my apologies.

Thanks to the team that help to make my books the very best they can be; Amanda Walker you killed it with the covers for this series. I'm so happy I found my way back to you after our first attempt because no one understands better what I want, and NO ONE delivers it better than you. #SuperSquirrel Extraordinaire is what you are and will always be to me. Kendra Gathier, thanks for making it look like I actually know where punctuation belongs and for helping me to keep growing as a writer with every book.

To my book girlfriends; Cindi Medley, April Moran, Nicole French, Andrea Bills, Christina Butrum, Cara Wade, Janine Bosco,

Laura Carr, Nicky Grant, Lili Mahoney, Patti West, and Taryn Steele, so glad this book world brought you into my life. It's a crazy little place and I'm so happy I have you close by to help make the journey a little easier.

Helene Cuji, thank you for your endless support and encouragement. You believed in me from day one and have been right beside me every step of the way since then. Your infectious laughter brightens my days, and the world around it.

To the bloggers and readers who read, review and share my posts, THANK YOU!!!! I appreciate you more than words can say for your endless devotion to spreading the word about books and authors you love. There are thousands of authors and stories, so to have you share my work is humbling and so very appreciated. Special thanks to Cindy Wolken, Nikki Pearce, Gina Moody, Cat Wright, Carolina Mamos, Jennifer Richey, Tiffany Brocato, Lyssa Dawn, All the IamaBookhoarder Girls, BookBistroBlog's Laura and Shabby, Inside_Neo's_World's Neomi, TalkBook's Mindy G., Panty Dropping Book Blog's Karrie Puskas, Reviews by Red's Dusty Summerford, all the Jewels in my group page, and last but not least, to my super fan, Natalie Jones, a.k.a. The Ninja.

~Trick~

I walk down the dimly lit hallway, ignoring anyone I pass along the way, my destination already decided before I even arrive. I tried to stay away tonight. I really did. I drank a quarter bottle of Patron in the hope I'd pass out into some kind of unconscious slumber in an attempt to stay away. It didn't work. I still couldn't shut out the images that played like a movie in my head every time I closed my eyes.

So, here I was, in the one place I knew I could lose myself. The one place I knew that could give me something else to focus on. Something else beside the demons always lurking in the recesses of my mind. Always reminding me that I shouldn't be here. I should be with them; burnt ash forever lost in the desert sands of Afghanistan.

I stop when I reach the entrance to my salvation, nodding at the door keeper. No one goes into this room unless they've been approved beforehand. His name is Gus and he knows me well enough to know that if I'm standing in front of this door, I'm in need of something more. More than I usually come looking for. He looks me up and down, his eyes cold and detached, and then nods. "Weren't you here just a couple days ago?"

"Yep." That's it. That's all he's getting unless he asks for more. It's my goddamn body to do whatever I want with.

"You even healed yet?" His eyes squint as he tries to assess my physical condition to see if I can handle what happens if he lets me through to the other side.

"I want more. I'm ready." I *need* more. I *crave* more. I *deserve* more.

He doesn't budge. It's a clear indication that my answer wasn't enough. I let out a long, slow breath through my nostrils and then pull my shirt over my head. I keep it clutched in my hand as I lift my arms out to my side and slowly turn in a circle, stopping when I'm facing him again.

"You've still got scabs." His eyes roaming over my chest.

"I'm fine." I reply, my voice flat and devoid of emotion.

He tilts his head once toward the door. My approval to enter. "Only because Mistress Blue doesn't mind a little bit of blood."

I keep my shirt off, clenching it in my hand as I walk by and push through the door. "Good, 'cause neither do I."

As soon as I'm on the other side, I take three steps to a padded black mat and fall to my knees, bowing my head as I rest my hands on the tops of my thighs. I've just given my submission to whomever wants it in this room. Any free will I had, any desires I had, any fear I had no longer exist or matter. They belong to someone else to control, to harness, to use in any way they want. For their pleasure, not mine. My only pleasure will be in the pain. And I prayed it was enough to make me forget for just a little while.

Goosebumps break out across my flesh when shiny, latex boots step into my vision, and then lock onto black fingernails clutched around the handle of a cat-o-nine tails. But this one isn't your typical whip. It's made of rope, instead of leather, and each end is knotted tightly. People think leather hurts, but the bite that rope takes out of your skin is so much more punishing. My cock twitches to life when she lifts it and then drags it across my bare back.

"Has Halloween come early?" Her sultry voice drips down to my ears. "I didn't even have to say Trick or Treat." She lowers herself, then turns the handle of the whip, placing it under my chin, lifting it until my eyes are even with hers. "My lucky day or yours?"

"Hopefully mine." Her brow quirks up at my reply as she stands, releasing the hold the handle has on my chin.

You can add Tempting Tricks to your Goodreads TBR here: https://www.goodreads.com/book/show/41434999-tempting-tricks

ABOUT THE AUTHOR

Michelle Windsor is a wife, mom, and a writer who lives North of Boston with her family. When she isn't writing, she's been known to partake in good wine and good food with her family and friends. She's a voracious reader, loves to hike with her German shepherd, Roman, enjoys a good romance movie and may be slightly obsessed with Outlander.

Stay up to date with Michelle on her website:
https://www.authormichellewindsor.com
or at any of the sites below:

f facebook.com/authormwindsor

🐦 twitter.com/Author_MWindsor

📷 instagram.com/author_michelle_windsor

BB bookbub.com/profile/michelle-windsor

ALSO BY MICHELLE WINDSOR

The Winning Bid, Auction Series Book One
The Final Bid, Auction Series Book Two
Losing Hope
Love Notes

Books Co-Authored with Haylee Thorne
Breaking Benjamin

Made in the USA
Middletown, DE
06 July 2021